**The crowd thickened around** them, **pushing** **closer together as people jostled to get a better place at the barrier. Callum wound his arm around her waist, holding her firmly against him to stop anyone coming between them. The countdown started.** *Ten, nine…*

It was the smallest of movements. Jess rested her head on his shoulder, then a few seconds later he felt her relax a little more and some of the weight of her body leaned next to his.

The grin spread across his face. It wasn't as if anyone could see it. But it was automatic and plastered there for the world to see. *Three, two, one…*

'Whoah!' The noise went around the crowd as the lights flickered on the Christmas tree, lighting up the square in a deluge of pink and silver.

'Pink! It's pink!' Jess yelped, as the wine sloshed out of her cup and she turned around to face him. Her eyes were sparkling, her excitement evident.

Her face was right in front of his, her brown eyes darker than ever before and their noses almost touching. He could see the steam from her breath in the cold night air.

He gave her a smile. 'My plan worked. I told them that pink was your favourite colour and that you'd be here.'

Her dark eyes were still sparkling, reflecting the twinkling lights around them. He could turn back the clock. He could flick a little switch right now and this could be thirteen years ago. Standing almost in this exact spot.

She tilted her head to the side. 'Well, that was a bit presumptuous, wasn't it?"

He shook his head. 'I don't think so. But this might be.'

He bent forward. People around them were still cheering about the Christmas lights, breaking into song as the music got louder through the amplifiers next to them.

But Callum wasn't noticing any of that. The only thing he was focused on was Jess's lips. And everything was just as he remembered. Almost as perfect.

Last time round Jess had tasted of strawberry lip gloss. This time she tasted of mulled wine. He could sense the tiniest bit of hesitation as he kissed her, so he took it slow. Gently kissing her lips, teasing at the edges, until she moved her hands from his shoulders and wrapped them around his neck, kissing him right back.

And then everything *was* perfect.

**Dear Reader**

This year has been a cause for celebration.

I celebrated a big birthday *(shh!)* in New York with my family, and two of my books were nominated for the Romantic Novelists' Association's RoNA Rose Award. I was delighted and honoured to have two Mills & Boon® Medical Romances™ on the shortlist, and to see the line that I love recognised.

This has also been the year I wrote my first non-medical hero. I'd like you all to meet Callum Kennedy, a firefighter in the rope rescue unit, who appeared fully-formed in my mind—and funnily enough in uniform! I also got to set my story in my nearest city—Glasgow.

Glasgow is gorgeous at Christmas time, with beautiful lights along Buchanan Street and on into George Square, with its ice rink and Christmas tree. Perfect for a Christmas story!

In this story Callum meets Jess—his childhood sweetheart—and he's shocked by the changes in her. Life has dealt Jess a cruel blow, and she's having a hard time recovering—but maybe Callum and his gorgeous son Drew can bring her all the Christmas cheer that she needs!

Please feel free to contact me at my website www.scarlet-wilson.com. I love to hear from readers!

Merry Christmas!

*Scarlet*

# HER FIREFIGHTER UNDER THE MISTLETOE

BY
SCARLET WILSON

First published in Great Britain 2013
by Mills & Boon, an imprint of Harlequin (UK) Limited.
Harlequin (UK) Limited, Eton House, 18-24 Paradise Road,
Richmond, Surrey TW9 1SR

© Scarlet Wilson 2013

ISBN: 978 0 263 23587 6

Harlequin (UK) policy is to use papers that are natural, renewable and recyclable products and made from wood grown in sustainable forests. The logging and manufacturing process conform to the legal environmental regulations of the country of origin.

Printed and bound in Great Britain
by CPI Antony Rowe, Chippenham, Wiltshire

**Scarlet Wilson** wrote her first story aged eight and has never stopped. Her family have fond memories of *Shirley and the Magic Purse*, with its army of mice, all with names beginning with the letter 'M'. An avid reader, Scarlet started with every Enid Blyton book, moved on to the *Chalet School* series and many years later found Mills & Boon®.

She trained and worked as a nurse and health visitor, and currently works in public health. For her, finding medical romances was a match made in heaven. She is delighted to find herself among the authors she has read for many years.

Scarlet lives on the West Coast of Scotland with her fiancé and their two sons.

**Recent titles by the same author:**

ABOUT THAT NIGHT…**
THE MAVERICK DOCTOR AND MISS PRIM**
AN INESCAPABLE TEMPTATION
HER CHRISTMAS EVE DIAMOND
A BOND BETWEEN STRANGERS*
WEST WING TO MATERNITY WING!
THE BOY WHO MADE THEM LOVE AGAIN
IT STARTED WITH A PREGNANCY

*The Most Precious Bundle of All
**Rebels with a Cause

**These books are also available in eBook format
from www.millsandboon.co.uk**

# CHAPTER ONE

Bzzz... bzzz...

The noise jerked Jess out of the delicious tranquil state that had been enveloping her.

Her eyes blinked at the bright light outside, the fuzziness of her brain trying to adjust and make sense of it all.

Her pager usually woke her in the dark of the night— just like it had three times last night. Having it wake her in the middle of the day was an entirely new experience.

A baby with RSV had kept her awake most of the night in Paediatric ITU, and when the ward had finally quietened down around an hour ago, she'd brought her coffee in here to do some paperwork.

Fat chance. She touched the coffee cup on her desk. Stone cold. Had she even managed a sip before she'd wiped out?

How long had she been asleep? She wriggled in her chair, rolling her shoulders back and trying to ease the knots out of her back.

Bzzz... Bzzz...

She glanced at the number. A and E. Another admission. Probably another respiratory problem.

It was Glasgow, at the start of November, but it felt like the middle of winter. The temperature had dropped dramatically in the last few days and paediatric emergency admissions had soared. Trips and falls on the slippery pavements had resulted in a whole host of strains, fractures and head injuries. Asthma and respiratory complaints were through the roof. Infections and nondescript viruses were causing mayhem with new babies and toddlers.

Just as well she didn't have anyone to go home to. She hadn't seen the inside of her house for days.

She picked up the phone and dialled A and E. 'It's Dr Rae. You were paging me.'

The voice was brusque, skipping over any pleasantries and getting straight to business. 'Assemble a flying squad. Nursery minibus in the Clyde on the city outskirts. Unknown number of casualties. We're waiting for more information from emergency services. You need to be ready to leave in five minutes.'

She was on her feet in seconds and throwing open the door, her tiredness, sore muscles and fatigue instantly forgotten. 'I need a flying squad,' she yelled, glancing down the corridor as the sister of the ward hurried towards her, 'Where's Jackie? I want her with me.'

Jackie appeared at her side in an instant. 'What is it?'

'Nursery minibus in the Clyde.'

The experienced nurse's face paled. 'In this weather? In these temperatures?'

'Go!' The ward sister waved her hand at them. 'Leave everything else to me.'

Jess started jogging down the corridor, heading for the stairs. It took less than a minute to reach A and E and one of the staff thrust a green suit into her hands. She climbed into it immediately, noting the fluorescent 'Doctor' sign on the back. It was essential that all staff could be picked out easily in an emergency. One of the paramedics thrust a pair of gloves towards her. 'Take these, you'll need them out there.'

She glanced at her watch. It was only two-thirty in the afternoon. At least a few hours of daylight left. She prayed they wouldn't need more than that.

'Let's go!'

The shout came from the front doors. Jackie appeared at her side again, similarly clad in a green jumpsuit with 'Nurse' emblazoned across the back. They picked up the pre-packed paediatric emergency kits and headed outside.

Jess climbed into one of the emergency vehicles and fastened her seat belt as the sirens sounded and they headed out onto the motorway. She turned to the man sitting next to her, 'I'm Jess, paediatric consultant. Have you heard any more?'

He nodded. 'Stan, emergency service co-ordinator. Lots of problems. Someone sideswiped the minibus and sent it down a thirty-foot slippery bank and straight into the Clyde.'

Jess tried to stop the sharp intake of breath. Her brain was into immediate overtime, imagining the types of injuries the children could have sustained.

'How many?'

He shook his head. 'Still waiting for confirmation. Three adults, at least ten kids.'

'Age range?'

'From two to five. We're getting more information all the time. The other nursery minibus missed everything. They didn't even know there had been an accident. The police are there now, collecting details of all the kids.'

Jess swallowed, trying to ignore the huge lump in her throat. The flying squad wasn't called out too often. She was the consultant on call—it was her job to be here. But that didn't mean her stomach wasn't churning at the thought of the scene she was about to face.

Yes, she could appear calm. Yes, she could use her skills

and clinical expertise. Yes, she would do everything that was expected of her and beyond.

But would she sleep tonight?

Probably not.

There was a crackle of the radio and some voices she couldn't distinguish. The driver turned his head. 'Five minutes. They've called out the rapid response and specialist rope rescue team. They should arrive just before us. Let's hope Callum got out of bed on the right side today.'

'Who is Callum?'

The words were out of her mouth automatically, before she even had a chance to think. 'And what's the specialist rope rescue team?'

None of this sounded good. All she could think about was the children involved in the crash. What did this mean for them?

Stan's face was pale. 'It means that the banking is too dangerous for our crews to work on, that, plus the added complication of being in water means we need the specialist crew.'

'Will it delay me getting to the children?'

Stan averted his eyes, obviously not wanting to give her the answer. He hadn't answered the other part of her question. He hadn't mentioned Callum. And the driver's comment had made her ears prick up. *Let's hope he got out of bed on the right side.*

The last thing she needed right now was a prima donna firefighter getting in her way when she had kids to attend to. 'Is Callum a bit on the crabbit side, then?' she asked as they pulled over to the side of the road. A bad-tempered man she could deal with. As long as he didn't interfere with her job.

'Only on a good day,' muttered Stan as he jumped from the rescue vehicle.

Jessica opened the door carefully, to avoid the passing traffic on the busy road. The police had cordoned part of it off as best they could. But the constant flow of traffic was unnerving.

The cold air hit her straight away. Biting cold, sneaking under the folds of her jumpsuit, made her wish she was wearing a hat, scarf and fleece and not just the thin gloves she'd been handed.

She flinched at the sight of the crash barrier, twisted beyond all recognition and lying like a useless piece of junk at the side of the road.

There were raised voices to her left. She turned just in time to see a broad-shouldered man snap on his harness and disappear down the side of the banking, with the vain words 'Risk assessment' being shouted after him by his colleagues.

A sense of unease came over her body. A vague awareness trickling through her. Callum—that's what they'd said. It couldn't possibly be Callum Kennedy, could it? She hadn't seen him since school and had no idea where he'd ended up. But there was something vaguely familiar about the body that had just disappeared over the edge.

Her footsteps shortened as she reached the edge of the steep bank. Someone touched her shoulder, looking at the sign on her back. 'Oh, good, the doctor. Let's get you harnessed up.'

She lifted her legs as she was clipped and harnessed and talked through the motions of the descent. Her bag was sent down ahead. A burly firefighter appeared next to her. 'You'll go down with me. Have you done this before?'

She peered over the edge again. Thirty feet of steep descent. How many times had the minibus rolled on the way down?

She could see it now, lying on its side in the Clyde,

the icy cold water surrounding it. There was a flurry of firefighters around it. Some on top, trying to get through the windows, some on the banking, surrounded by other pieces of equipment.

'Get me down there.' Her eyes met the firefighter's and the whispered words grew more determined. 'Get me down to those children.'

He nodded and spoke into the radio clipped to his shoulder. 'The doc and I are on our way.'

She took a deep breath and turned with her back towards the water, edging down the side of the bank in time with the firefighter. It was slippery work. A thin layer of frost had formed over the mud at the side of the bank, her simple shoes giving her literally no grip. The firefighter's firm hand in the small of her back kept her from slipping completely. Even through her gloves the biting cold was already making her fingers numb.

She looked over her shoulder. 'How much further?'

'Keep your eyes straight ahead, please.'

Her anxiety was building. She wanted to get down. She wanted to help those kids. But she needed to get down there in one piece.

'Who is Callum? Is it Callum Kennedy?'

The firefighter's eyes gave a spark of amusement. 'Know him, do you?'

She wrinkled her nose. 'I'm not entirely sure. I think so. I went to school with a Callum Kennedy, but I didn't get a good look at him before he went over the edge.' She shrugged her shoulders, 'I'm not even sure he would recognise me now.'

The firefighter gave her a little smile, 'Oh, I'm sure he would.'

'What does he do exactly?'

'He's the head of the rope rescue unit. He'll be in charge

down here.' They were inching closer and closer to the bottom.

'And is he any good?' She bit her lip. It might seem a little cheeky, but Stan had already mentioned he could be crabbit. She needed to know that he wouldn't get in her way. That he wouldn't stop her doing her job with these kids.

'Put it this way—if me or my kids were stuck anywhere that a rope rescue was needed?' He lifted his eyes skyward. 'I would be praying to the man upstairs that Callum would be on duty that night. He's the safest pair of hands we've got—particularly near kids.' He caught her around the waist. 'That's us. Let me just unhook you from this line—but we'll leave your harness on. You'll need it to get back up and they'll hook you up to another one if you're near the water.'

'Where's the doc?' came the shout.

Jess swivelled around, looking for her bag. 'I'm here. I'm coming.'

Several of the firefighters were forming a line, passing two little kids along to the edge of the bank. Jackie appeared at her side. 'Let's go.'

They reached the kids just as they were placed on warm blankets on the ground. Jess worked quickly, gently feeling over their little bodies for signs of injuries as she spoke to them in a quiet voice.

'Need some help?'

She nodded at the firefighter next to her. 'Heat them up. There are no obvious injuries. But they're in shock.' She turned back to the minibus. Now she was closer she could see every dent, every bash, every hole in the metalwork.

It made the chill seem even worse. 'Are these the first two?'

The man next to her nodded. 'Do we have a number yet? How many kids are injured?'

'Twelve. That's the figure we have for the moment. Just awaiting confirmation.'

She moved over to the side of the slippery river's edge as an adult was passed along and dealt with by the paramedics. She could see the hive of activity going on within the bus, hear the whimpering cries of the children.

'Can I get over there? Do you need me to get into the bus?' Her anxiety was building. She couldn't stand here and do nothing. It just wasn't in her nature. She needed to be at the heart of the action. It was her job to prioritise, triage and treat the sickest kids. She needed to be next to those children.

Her voice must have carried in the cold air, because a head whipped up from the bus. The man was lying across the windows, reaching down to grasp a squirming child, and his eyes connected with hers.

'Stay *exactly* where you are.'

Callum. Callum Kennedy. Absolutely no mistake.

She saw him flinch visibly as his brain made the connection of who was standing on the riverbank.

He'd recognised her? After all these years?

The cold hard air hit her lungs. She must have sucked in a bigger breath than normal. Her skin prickled.

How did she feel about seeing Callum Kennedy thirteen years on?

Unprepared.

Like a seventeen-year-old again, standing in a dark nightclub and willing herself not to cry as they broke up. It had been the right decision. The sensible decision. They had both been going to university, she in Glasgow and he—after a wait of a few years—in Aberdeen. Their relationship would never have worked out. It had been best for them both.

It just hadn't felt that way.

She pushed her feet more firmly into the ground, trying to focus her attention. Callum's gaze hadn't moved. It was still fixed on her face.

She could feel the colour start to rise in her cheeks. It was unnerving. But why the flinch? Was she really such an unwelcome sight after all this time?

Or maybe she was imagining this—maybe he'd no idea who she was at all.

Callum couldn't believe it. He was holding a child firmly by the waist, while a colleague released him from his seat belt.

But Callum's eyes were fixed on the flyaway caramel-coloured hair on the riverbank. Running up and down the thin frame that was in no way hidden by the bright green jumpsuit.

A sight he hadn't seen in thirteen years.

A lifetime ago.

His childhood sweetheart, here on the banks of the Clyde, at the scene of an accident.

He'd always wondered if he'd come across her sometime, some place.

As a firefighter he'd been in and out of most of the A and E departments in the city. But in all these years he'd never glimpsed her, never seen her name on any board.

He knew that Jessica had gone to university to do her medical training, but had no idea where she'd ended up, or which field she'd specialised in.

And now he knew. She was somewhere here in Glasgow, specialising in paediatrics. Why else would she be here?

Would she even remember him? It looked as though she had—even though he'd filled out considerably since the last time they'd met. She, on the other hand, looked as if she'd faded away to a wisp.

Although he could see her slight frame, the most visible changes were around her facial features and structure. And it wouldn't have mattered how many clothes she was bundled up in, he would have noticed at twenty paces.

It struck him as strange. The young Jessica he remembered had had an attention-grabbing figure and a personality to match. Every memory he had of her was a happy one. And for a second he felt as if they could all come flooding back.

There was a tug at his arms, followed by a sensation of relief and a lightening of the weight in his arms. He pulled upwards automatically. The little guy's seat belt had been released.

He pulled him up and held him to his chest, capturing the little body with his own, holding him close to let a little heat envelop the shivering form. The little boy wasn't even crying any more. He was just too cold.

He held the boy for a few seconds longer. He looked around four, just a year younger than his own son Drew. He couldn't help the automatic paternal shiver that stole down his spine at the thought of something like this happening to his son. It didn't even bear thinking about.

His only relief right now was that he hadn't signed a consent form for the school to go on any trips this week, meaning that his little Drew was safely tucked up inside the primary school building.

The temperature in the minibus was freezing, with water halfway up its side-on frame. They were going to have to move quicker to get these kids out in time.

'Callum! Callum! Pass him over, please.'

Oh, she'd recognised him all right. The authoritative tone made no mistake about that.

'Okay, little guy, we're going to get you heated up now.' He ruffled the little boy's hair before he passed him over to the arms stretched out towards him. He didn't have time to think about Jessica Rae now. Too much was at stake.

He thrust his head back inside the minibus. 'How are we doing?'

John, one of his co-workers, lifted his head. 'I'll have two more for you in a second. But I need some more light in here.'

Another voice shouted from the darkness, 'I think I've got one with a broken leg and another unconscious. Can we get a paramedic or a doctor in here?'

Callum lifted his head back up. The light was fading quickly, even though it was only afternoon. Winter nights closed in quickly—by four p.m. it would be pitch black. He didn't think twice. 'I need a paramedic or a doctor over here, please.'

He could see the quick confab at the side of the river. Jess was issuing instructions to the nurse with her and the paramedics and ambulance technicians at her side. Things were going smoothly out there. Two of the children and one of the adults had already been transported back up the slippery bank. The latest little guy was still being assessed.

Jess moved to the side of the bank. He could see the impatience on her face as she waited for her safety harness to be clipped to the harness point on the shore. She shook her head at the waders she was offered, grabbed at a hand that was offered and started to climb towards the minibus.

It was precarious. The Clyde was not a quiet-flowing river. It was fast and churning, the icy-cold water lapping furiously at the side of the minibus as it penetrated the interior.

The minibus was moving with the momentum of the river and Jess slipped as she climbed over the wing of the minibus, the weight from her pack making her unstable. She was just within Callum's reach and he stretched out and grabbed the tips of her fingers with a fierce, claw-like grip.

'Yeowww!' Her other hand flailed upwards then closed over his, and he steadied her swaying body as she thudded down next to him.

The red colour in her cheeks was gone, replaced with the whiteness of cold. 'Thanks,' she breathed, the warm air forming a little steamy cloud next to them.

'Fancy seeing you here,' he murmured, giving her a little smile. It had been impossible to spot from the riverbank, but here, up close, he had a prime-time view of the thing he'd always loved most about Jess—her deep brown eyes.

The smile was returned. That little acknowledgement.

That in another time, another place…

The memories were starting to invade his senses. Jessica in his arms throwing back her head and laughing, exposing the pale skin of her neck—skin that he wanted to touch with his lips.

His brain kicked back into gear. This was work. And he never got distracted at work.

'Have you done anything like this before?'

She pulled back a little. It was the tiniest movement, a flinch almost, as if she was taken aback by his change of tone.

She shook her head and her eyebrows rose. 'An overturned minibus in a fast-flowing river with lots of paediatric casualties?'

The irony wasn't lost on him. He might do this sort of thing day in, day out, but Jess was usually in the confines of a safe, warm, comfortable hospital.

She hunched up onto her knees and pointed at the harness. 'I've never even had one of these on before, let alone abseiled down a hillside.' She wiggled her hips and tried to move her tether. 'These things aren't too comfortable, are they?'

It struck him—almost blindsided him—how brave she was being. The Jessica Rae he'd known at school hadn't even liked contact sports. He closed his eyes as an unguarded memory of other activities of a physical nature swam into his mind.

Focus. Focus now.

He knelt upwards and grabbed her around her waist, trying not to think about how it felt to be touching Jessica Rae again after all these years. Trying not to remember how her firm flesh used to feel beneath his fingers. What had happened?

'I'm going to lower you down, Jess.' He peered through the side window next to them, which had been removed. 'Your feet will get a bit wet because there's some water on the floor. Are you okay with that?'

She nodded. She didn't look scared. She didn't look panicked. But there was a tiny little flicker of something behind her eyes. She looked in control.

He shouted down into the minibus. 'John, I'm going to lower the doc down. Can you take care of her?'

She started. 'Take care of me?' It was almost as if he'd just insulted her. 'Don't you mean take care of the kids?'

But Callum wasn't paying attention. He was back in rescue mode. 'There are two kids in the back who need your attention. One unconscious, the other with a broken leg. It's too cramped in there to take your bag down. Shout up and tell me what you need.'

Their eyes met again as she shrugged off her pack. 'Ready?' She nodded and he lowered her down slowly into the waiting arms of the firefighter below, praying that things would go to plan.

* * *

'Sheesh!' Her feet hit the icy cold water and it sent the surge of cold right up through her body. No one could stand in this for long.

It took her eyes a few seconds to adjust to the gloom inside the minibus. The mottled daylight was still sending shadows through one side of the bus, but Callum's body and those of the other firefighters lying across the windows was blocking out the little light that was left.

A flashlight was thrust into her hands. 'Here you go, Doc.' She turned it on immediately. The first sight was the way the water was lapping quickly around them. She felt the vaguest wave of panic. 'Is the river rising?'

John nodded. 'Not quickly enough for us to worry about.' His eyes didn't quite meet hers.

Work quickly.

She noticed his black trousers ballooning around his ankles and gave him a little nod. 'Did you say no to the waders too?'

He smiled. 'No room for waders in here, Doc. Space is limited.'

She nodded and she shuffled around him towards the kids. 'Are any of the kids in water?' Her feet were already numb. There was a real danger of hypothermia setting in for any kid exposed to these temperatures.

'Four.'

'Four?' She could feel a flare of panic. She was one person. How could she attend to four kids?

Callum stuck his head in the gap. 'Start with the two at the back, Jess. As soon as you've stabilised them and they're safe to move, my men will get them out. The other two don't appear injured.' He pointed to the front of the bus. 'My men are getting them out as quickly as possible.'

He looked towards the back of the bus. 'The little girl is called Rosie.'

His voice was calm, authoritative. The kind of guy in an emergency who told you things would be okay and you believed him—just because of the way he said it.

She pushed her way back to a little girl with masses of curly hair, still strapped into her seat. Her leg was at a peculiar angle, and it hadn't taken a doctor to make an accurate diagnosis of a fracture. The little boy behind her, strapped into the window seat, was unconscious, but she couldn't possibly get to him until she'd moved this little girl. She took off her gloves and put her hand round the girl, feeling for a pulse at his neck and checking to see he was still breathing. Yes, his pulse was slowing and his chest was rising and falling. But in these cold temperatures hypothermia was a real risk. She had to work as quickly as possible.

The water was lapping around their little legs and would be dropping their temperatures dramatically.

She shouted up to Callum, 'I need you to pass me down the kit with analgesia—I need to give Rosie some morphine. It's in a red box, in the front pouch of the bag.' She waited a few seconds until the box appeared then shouted again, 'And an inflatable splint.'

She spoke gently to Rosie, stroking her hair and distracting her, calculating the dosage in her head. It was too difficult to untangle the little girl from her clothes and find an available patch of skin. The last thing she needed to do was cause this little girl more pain. She took a deep breath and injected it through the thick tights on her leg, waiting a few minutes for it to take effect. 'Pass me the splint,' she whispered to John.

The positioning on the bus was difficult. 'I'm sorry, honey,' she whispered, as the little girl gave a little yelp as she straightened her leg and inflated the splint around about it to hold it in place.

'Is she ready to be moved?'

'Not quite. Can you get a collar? In fact, get me two. Once I've got that on her, you can move her.'

It was only a precaution. The little girl didn't appear to have any other injuries apart from her leg. She seemed to be moving her other limbs without any problems, but Jess didn't want to take a risk.

It only took a few seconds to manoeuvre the collar into place and fasten it securely. The cold water was moving quickly. It had only been around the children's legs when she'd entered the vehicle—now it was reaching their waists. Time was absolutely of the essence here.

She was freezing. How on earth would these children be feeling? Kids were so much more susceptible to hypothermia because they lost heat more quickly than adults.

Another firefighter had appeared next to John, and they held a type of stretcher between them. Space was at a premium so Jess pushed herself back into the corner of the bus to allow them to load the little girl and pass her up through the window to Callum.

Time was ticking on. The sky was darkening and the level of the freezing water rising. She squeezed her way into the seat vacated by the little girl and started to do a proper assessment on the little unconscious boy, who was held in place by his seat belt.

'Anyone know his name?' she shouted to the crew.

'It's Marcus.' The deep voice in her ear made her jump.

'Where did you come from? I thought you were on the roof?'

'The water's too cold to have anyone in it for long. I told John to go ashore and dry off.'

'Tell me about it. Try being a kid.'

There was an easy familiarity in having Callum at her side. It didn't matter that she hadn't seen him for years, it almost felt as if it had been yesterday.

Callum had changed, and so had she. The skinny youth had filled out in all the right places. His broad shoulders and muscled chest were visible through his kit. The shorter hairstyle suited him—even though it revealed the odd grey hair. They were only visible this close up.

'What do you need?'

He was watching as she checked Marcus's pulse, took his temperature, looked him over for any other injuries and shone a torch in his eyes to check his pupil reactions.

She shook her head. 'This is going to have to be a scoop and run. He's showing severe signs of hypothermia. His pulse is low and I can't even get a reading with this thing.' She shook the tympanic thermometer in the air. 'So much for accurate readings.'

She placed the collar around his neck. 'I don't want to waste any time. I can't find an obvious reason for him being unconscious. His clothes are soaking—right up to his chest. We can't waste another second. Can you get me some kind of stretcher so we can get him out of here?'

Callum nodded. 'Get me a basket stretcher,' he shouted to one of his colleagues. He gestured his head to the side as the stretcher was passed down. She stared at the orange two-piece contraption, watching while he took a few seconds to slot the pins into place and assemble it. It had curved sides, handholds, adjustable patient restraints and a lifting bridle.

'This is the only way we'll get the casualties back up the steep embankment. Jump back up, Jess, we need as much room as we can to manipulate this into place.' A pair of strong arms reached down through the window to-wards her and she grabbed them willingly. It pained her to leave the little boy's side, but there wasn't time for egos or arguments here.

The cold air hit her again as she came back out into the open. If she'd thought standing in the icy water had been bad, it was nothing compared to the wind-chill factor. Her teeth started chattering.

'How…many more patients?' she asked the firefighter next to her.

'We've extricated all the adults. There's another two kids stuck behind the front seat, but their injuries are minor and they're not in contact with the water. We'll get to them next.'

'Has someone looked them over?'

He nodded. 'Your nurse and one of the paramedics. They had another kid who was submerged. She'll be in the ambulance ahead of you. We've just radioed in.'

The minibus gave another little lurch as the currents buffeted it. 'This thing had better not roll,' came the mumble from next to her.

Jess wobbled, trying to gain her balance. She hadn't even considered the possibility of the bus rolling. That would be a nightmare. There was a tug around her waist, and she looked to the side of the riverbank where one of the rope crew was taking up some of the slack in her line. The stretcher started to emerge through the window. At last. Maybe she'd get a better look at Marcus out here.

Callum's shoulders appeared. He was easing the stretcher up gently, guiding it into the arms of his colleagues.

The minibus lurched again. Callum disappeared back down into the depths of the minibus with a thud and a matching expletive. The firefighter next to her struggled to steady the weight in his arms, the stretcher twisting and its edge catching her side-on.

She teetered at the edge of the bus, losing her footing on the slippery side.

It seemed to happen in slow motion. She felt herself fall backwards, her arms reaching out in front of her. The firefighter who'd knocked her with the stretcher had panic written all over his face. There was a fleeting second as he struggled to decide whether to decide to grab her or maintain his hold on the stretcher.

What was it that knocked the air from her lungs? The impact of hitting the water? Or the icy water instantly closing over her head? Her reaction was instantaneous, sucking inwards in panic, instead of holding her breath.

The layers of clothes were weighing her down, as were her shoes. She tried to reach for the surface. The water hadn't been that deep, had it? She was choking. Trying to suck in air that wasn't there—only murky water. Then the overwhelming feeling of panic started to take over.

# CHAPTER TWO

CALLUM HIT THE bottom of the river-filled minibus with a thud, the icy water doing nothing to slow the impact. What little part of him had remained dry was now soaked to the skin.

There was a splash outside, followed by some panicked shouts. Callum was instantly swept with a feeling of dread. The jolt had been a big one. *Please, don't let them have dropped the stretcher.*

He was on his feet in seconds, his arms grabbing at the window edge above him and pulling himself up onto the side of the bus.

The stretcher was steady, the child safe and being passed along the line. The crew around him, however, was panicking.

'Where's her line? Wasn't she wearing a line?'

Oh, no. His head flicked from side to side, searching frantically for any sign of Jess. She was the only female river-side. Everyone else was safely ashore. They could only be talking about her.

'Can you see her? Can anyone see her?'

Callum didn't hesitate. Not for a second. He saw where the outstretched fingers were pointing and jumped straight into the Clyde.

The water closed around his chest, leaving him up to his

neck with barely a toehold on the river's bed. Even after the water in the minibus, being fully submerged in the fast-flowing Clyde was a shock to the system. Every part of his body seemed to react at once. Everything went on full alert, hairs on end, trying to pull heat back into his centre.

He looked around him, shouting at the guys still on top of the bus. 'Where? Here?' He pointed to the riverbank. 'Tell them to pull in her line!'

The Clyde was murky and grey and several pieces of ice, broken from the river's edge, floated past.

He swept his arms around under the water. He couldn't see a thing. Not even a flash of the bright green jumpsuit she'd been wearing. The water wasn't too deep as he was on tiptoe. But he was a good foot taller than Jess, with a lot more bulk and muscle. Even he could feel the hidden currents pulling at his weight.

Every man working on the minibus had been wearing a line—except him. He took a few seconds to follow the lines from the riverbank to the bus, until he located the one that led directly into the river.

The firefighters on the bank were having the same problem. It took a few moments of frantic scrambling to ascertain which line belonged to Jess. They started to reel it in and Callum waded through the water towards it.

There! A flash of green as she was tugged nearer the surface.

He grabbed, lifting her whole body with one arm, raising her head and chest above the water's surface.

For the briefest second there was nothing, just the paler-than-pale face.

Then she coughed and spluttered, and was promptly sick into the river. He fastened one arm around her chest, pulling her back towards him, supporting her weight and lifting his other arm to signal to the crew to stop pulling in her line.

'I've got you, Jess. It's okay.' He whispered the words calmly in her ear. The cold wasn't bothering him now. There was no heat coming from her body, but he could feel the rise and fall of her chest under his hands. He could feel her breathe.

Relief. That was the sensation sweeping through him. Pure and utter relief.

He always felt like this after a rescue. It was as if the anxiety and stomach-clenching that had been an essential part of his momentum and drive to keep going just left him all at once. More often than that, after a rescue he would go home and sleep soundly for ten hours, all his energy expended. Building reserves for the next day so he could do it all again.

Even Drew understood. And on those nights his little body would climb into bed next to his father and cuddle in, his little back tucked against Callum's chest—just the way Jess's was now.

She coughed and spluttered again. He could hear her teeth chattering. She still hadn't spoken. Was she in shock?

There would be an investigation later. An investigation into why the paediatric consultant helping them had ended up in the middle of a fast-flowing icy river.

But right now he wanted to make sure Jess was okay. He started wading towards the riverbank, keeping Jess close to his chest. Several of his colleagues waded in towards him, sweeping Jess out of his arms and wrapping them both in blankets.

One of the paramedics started pulling out equipment to check her over. Callum pulled his jacket and shirt over his head. The cold air meant nothing to him right now—

he couldn't be any colder anyway. He gratefully accepted a red fleece thrust at him by one of his colleagues.

He pulled it over his head. There was instant heat as soft fleece came into contact with his icy skin. Bliss.

Two basket stretchers with a firefighter on either side were currently being guided up the steep, treacherous slope. The two kids with hypothermia. He could see the ambulance technicians waiting at the top of the bank, ready to load them into the waiting ambulances.

'Stop it!'

He turned, just in time to see Jess push herself to her feet and take a few wobbly steps.

'I'm fine. Now, leave me alone.' She pulled the blankets closer around her, obviously trying to keep the cold out.

He turned to one of his colleagues. 'See if someone will volunteer some dry clothing for our lady doc.'

Jess stalked towards him. Her face was still deathly pale, but her involuntary shivering seemed to have stopped. She pointed to the stretchers. 'I need to get to the kids. I need to get them to hospital.'

Callum shook his head. 'Jess, you've just been submerged in freezing water. You need to get checked over yourself. The kids will go straight to Parkhill. One of your colleagues will be able to take care of them.'

She shook her head fiercely. '*I* will take care of them. I'm the consultant on call. Neither of my junior colleagues has enough experience to deal with this. Two kids with hypothermia? It's hardly an everyday occurrence. Those kids need me right now.'

One of the firefighters appeared at his side with a T-shirt and another jacket. Callum rolled his eyes. 'You've still got a stubborn streak a mile wide, haven't you?'

He handed the clothes over to her. 'Get changed and I'll get you back topside.' She shrugged off her jumpsuit, tying the wet top half around her middle, hesitating only for a second before she pulled her thin cotton top off underneath.

In just a few seconds he saw her pale skin and the outline of her small breasts against her damp white bra. It was almost translucent. She pulled the other T-shirt over her head in a flash. But not before he'd managed to note just how thin she was.

Jess had always been slim. But slim with curves. What had happened to her?

She zipped the jacket up to her neck. Meeting his eyes with a steely glare. Daring him to mention the fact she'd just stripped at a riverside, or to mention her obviously underweight figure.

Callum knew better.

He'd learned over the last few years to pick his battles carefully.

Now wasn't the time.

He signalled and a couple of lines appeared down the side of the steep incline. He leaned over and clipped her harness. Her whole bottom half was still wet—as was his. Spare T-shirts and jackets could be found, but spare shoes and trousers? Not a chance.

'You do realise we go back up the way we came down?'

She sighed, but he couldn't help but notice the faint tremble in her hands. An after-effect of the cold water? Or something else?

He stepped behind her and interlocked their harnesses. 'The quickest way to get you back up is to let me help you.'

He could see her brain searching for a reason to disagree.

'You want to get back up to those kids?'

She nodded. Whatever her reservations, she'd pushed them aside.

'Then let me help you. It's like abseiling in reverse. Lean back against me.'

She was hesitating, still keeping all the weight on her legs, so he pulled her backwards towards him. He felt a little shock to feel her body next to his.

It had felt different in the water, more buoyant, the water between them cushioning the sensation. But now it was just clothes. Wet clothes, which clung to every curve of their bodies.

Her body was tense, stiff, and it took a few seconds for her to relax. He wrapped his arms around her, holding onto the lines in front of them, and gave them a little tug. His lips accidentally brushed against her ear as he spoke to her. 'We let the lines take our weight. If you just lean back into me, I'll walk up back up the incline. Just try and keep your legs in pace with mine. It feels a little weird, but it'll only take a few minutes.'

He let her listen, digest his words. He could feel her breathing sync with his, the rise and fall of their chests becoming simultaneous. She put her hands forward, holding onto the same line as he was, reaching for a little security in the strange situation.

He wrapped his hands around hers. His thick gloves were in place, to take the taut strain of the line.

He felt the tug of the line and started to walk his legs up the slope, taking her weight on his body. He looked skyward. Praying for divine intervention to stop any reactions taking place.

It was the weirdest sensation. The last time their bodies had been locked together she'd been seventeen and he'd been twenty-one. A whole lifetime had passed since then.

A marriage, a divorce, a fierce custody battle—and that was just him. What had happened to her?

His eyes went automatically to her hand. He'd always

imagined a girl like Jess would be happily married with a couple of kids by this age. But even through her wet gloves he could see there was no outline of a wedding band. Not even an engagement ring.

Something clenched at him. Was it curiosity? Or was it some strange thrill that Jess might be unattached?

His head was buzzing. He couldn't even make sense of his thoughts. He hadn't seen this woman in years. He hadn't even *heard* about her in years. He had no idea what life had flung at Jessica Rae. And she had no idea what life had thrown at him.

Drew. The most important person in his world.

A world he kept tightly wrapped and carefully preserved.

Drew's mother, Kirsten, had left after the divorce and costly custody battle. She was in New York—married to her first love, who she'd claimed she should never have left in the first place, as he was twice the man that Callum was. Callum had been a 'poor substitute'. Words that still stung to this day.

By that point, Callum couldn't have cared less about her frequent temper tantrums and outbursts. He had only cared about how they impacted on Drew.

Drew was the best and only good thing to have come out of that marriage.

He didn't intend to make the same mistake twice.

He'd never introduced any woman to Drew in the three years following his divorce. No matter how many hints they'd dropped.

But his immediate and natural curiosity was taking over. He didn't have a single bad memory about Jessica Rae. Even their break-up had been civilised.

Seeing her today had been a great shock, but her warm brown eyes and loose curls took him straight back thirteen years and he couldn't resist the temptation to find out a little more when it was just the two of them. They were around halfway up now. 'So, how have you been, Jessica? It's been a long time since we were in a position like this.'

He was only half-joking. Trying to take some of the strain out of her muscles, which had tensed more and more as they'd ascended the slope. Was Jessica scared of heights?

Her voice was quiet—a little thoughtful even. 'Yes. It has been, hasn't it?' She turned her head a little so he could see the side of her face. 'I'd no idea you were a firefighter. Didn't you do engineering at uni?'

She'd remembered. Why did that seem important to him?

'Yes, three years at Aberdeen Uni.' He gave a fake shudder. 'These would be normal temperatures for up there.'

'So, how did you end up being a firefighter?'

Was she just being polite? Or was she genuinely curious? He'd probably never know.

'There was a fire in the student accommodation where I stayed. We were on the tenth floor.' He tried to block out the pictures in his mind. 'It gave me a whole new perspective on the fire service. They needed to call out a specialist team and specialist equipment to reach us.' He didn't normally share this information with people. But Jess was different. Jess knew him in ways that most other people didn't.

'That must have been scary.'

Not even close. There was so much he was leaving unsaid.

The terrifying prospect of being marooned on a roof with the floors beneath you alight.

The palpable terror of the students around you.

The look on the faces of the fire crew when they realised you were out of reach and they had to stand by and wait, helpless, until other crew and equipment arrived.

'Callum?'

'What? Oh, yes, sorry. Let's just say it made me appreciate the engineering work involved in the fire service's equipment. I joined when I finished university. It didn't take me long to find my calling at the rope rescue unit. I still do some other regular firefighting duties, but most of the time I'm with the rescue unit.' He wanted to change the subject. He didn't want her to ask any questions about the fire. 'What about you? Are you married with four kids by now?'

It was meant to be simple. A distraction technique. A simple change of subject, taking the emphasis off him and putting it back on to her.

But as soon as the words left his mouth he knew he'd said the wrong thing. The stiffness and tension in her muscles was automatic.

They were nearing the edge of the incline and he could see movement above them. The flurry of activity as the stretchers were pulled over the edge and the paramedics and technicians started dealing with the children.

'Things just didn't work out for me.'

Quiet words, almost whispered.

He was stunned into silence.

There was obviously much more to it than that but now was hardly the time or the place.

And who was he to be asking?

He hadn't seen Jessica in thirteen years. Was it any of his business what had happened to her?

The radio on his shoulder crackled into life. 'We've got the last two kids. Minor injuries—nothing significant. There's an ambulance on standby that will take them to be checked over.'

'Are all the ambulances heading to Parkhill?' She sounded anxious.

He lifted the radio to his mouth. 'Wait and I'll check. Control—are all paediatric patients being taken to Parkhill?'

There was a buzz, some further crackles, then a disjointed voice. 'Four classified as majors, eight as minors. Two majors and six minors already en route. The adults have gone to Glasgow Cross.'

'Give me your hand!' A large arm reached over the edge and grabbed Jessica's wrist, pulling them topside. Someone unclipped their harnesses and tethers, leaving them free of each other.

'Doc, you're requested in one of the ambulances.'

Jess never even turned back, just started running towards the nearest ambulance, where one of the hypothermic kids was being loaded.

Callum watched her immediately fall back into professional mode.

'Scoop and run,' she shouted. 'Get that other ambulance on the move and someone get me a line to Parkhill. I want them to be set up for our arrival.'

Callum looked around him. The major incident report was going to be a nightmare. It would probably take up the next week of his life.

He grabbed hold of the guy next to him. 'Any other problems?'

The guy shook his head. 'Just waiting to lock and load the last two kids. The clean-up here will take hours.'

Callum nodded. 'In that case, I'm going to Parkhill with the ambulances. I want to find out how all these kids do. I'll be back in a few hours.'

He jumped into the back of one of the other ambulances, where the paramedic and nurse were treating the other hypothermic kid. 'Can I hitch a ride?' He glanced at the nurse, who was balanced on one leg. 'Did you hurt yourself?'

The paramedic nodded.

'Ride up front with the technician. We're going to be busy back here.'

The nurse grimaced, looking down at her leg. 'I'm sure it's nothing. Let's just get these kids back to Parkhill.'

Callum jumped back down and closed the doors, sliding into the passenger seat at the front. Within seconds the ambulance had taken off, sirens blaring. Great, the paediatrician had ended up in the Clyde and the nurse had injured her ankle. The major incident report was getting longer by the second.

It wouldn't take long to get through the city traffic at this time. He pulled his notebook from his top pocket. It was sodden. Useless, soaked when the minibus had tipped and he'd landed in the water.

'Got anything I can write on?'

The technician nodded, his eyes never leaving the road, and gestured his head towards the glove box, where Callum found a variety of notebooks and pens.

'Perfect. Thanks.' He started scribbling furiously. It was essential he put down as much as could for the incident report, before it became muddled in his brain.

The number of staff in attendance. The number of victims. The decision to call out the medical crew. Jessica. The descent down the incline. The temperature and depth of the water. Jessica being called onto the minibus. His first impression of the casualties. The way the casualties had been prioritised. The fact that Jessica had landed in the water.

The feeling in his chest when she'd disappeared under the water.

He laid the notebook and pen down in his lap.

This was no use.

He wasn't thinking the way he usually did. Calmly. Methodically.

He just couldn't get her out of his head.

It seemed that after thirteen years of immunity Jessica had reclaimed her place—straight back under his skin.

# CHAPTER THREE

THE AMBULANCE DOORS were flung open and Jess heaved a sigh of relief. Her team was ready and waiting.

The A and E department would be swamped. There were twelve kids with a variety of injuries to look after, as well as all the normal walking wounded patients and GP emergency admissions that would have turned up today.

Everyone would be on edge. The place would be going like a fair.

Her team sprang into action immediately as she jumped down from the ambulance.

'Is the resus room set up for these two kids?'

'All prepared, Dr Rae. Fluids heating as we speak. Harry Shaw, the anaesthetist, and Blake Connor, the registrar, will help you run these kids simultaneously. You're drookit, Jess. Wanna get changed?'

A set of scrub trousers were thrust into her hands and she gave a little smile. Her team had thought of everything.

Harry appeared at her side. 'I take it it was freezing out there?'

'Baltic.' The one-word answer told him everything he needed to know.

The second ambulance arrived and both kids were wheeled into the resus room and transferred to the trolleys. Jess ducked behind a curtain and shucked off her soggy jumpsuit, replacing it the with the dry scrub trousers. If only her underwear wasn't still sodden.

Her team was on autopilot, stripping the freezing-wet clothing from both kids and bundling them up in warming blankets.

She walked out from behind the curtains. Harry Shaw was standing at the head of one of the trolleys, doing his initial assessment. 'What can you tell me?'

She looked up as Callum appeared at the doorway and handed her a sheet of paper. 'Thought this might be useful,' he said as he walked away.

She stared at what he'd scribbled for her. *Temperature of the Clyde is currently minus five degrees centigrade. Moving water takes longer to freeze.*

It was just what she needed. The temperature to which these kids had been exposed was very important.

She walked over to Harry. 'This is Marcus, he's four. He was unconscious at the scene but I can't find any obvious sign of injury. Showing severe signs of hypothermia. As far as I know, his head was always above the water, but we couldn't get the tympanic thermometer to register on-site.'

Harry nodded. 'I need baseline temps on both these kids. Has to be a core temperature, so oesophageal temperatures would be best.'

More paperwork appeared in her hand from the receptionist. 'Nursery just called with some more details.'

Her eyes scanned the page and she let out a little sigh. 'This is Lily. She's four too. She was submerged at the scene—but no one can be sure how long.'

Harry was one of the most experienced paediatric anaesthetists that she knew. He'd already realised that Lily was the priority and left Connor to take over with Marcus. He was already sliding an ET tube into place for Lily. He took a few seconds to check her temperature. Both cardiac monitors were switched on and the team stood silently to watch them flicker to life.

Jessica's heart thumped in her chest. What happened in the next few minutes would determine whether these kids made it or not.

'Marcus's temp is thirty degrees. Moderate hypothermia,' shouted Connor.

She watched the monitor for a few more seconds. 'He's bradycardic but his cardiac rhythm appears stable. Any problems with his breathing?'

Connor shook his head. 'He's maintaining his airway. His breathing's just slowed along with his heart rate.'

Jessica's brain was racing. She was the paediatric consultant. This was her lead. But Harry was an extremely experienced anaesthetist. She wanted to be sure they were on the same page.

She turned to him. 'Warmed, humidified oxygen, contact rewarming with a warming unit, rewarmed IV fluids and temperature monitoring. Do you agree?'

He gave her a little smile over the top of his glasses. 'Sounds like a plan. I've paged one of my other anaesthetists to come down.' The nursing staff started to flurry around them, carrying out the instructions. Jessica felt nervous.

Hypothermia was more common in elderly patients than in children. Every year they had a few cases come through the doors of A and E, but she wasn't always on duty. And most of those kids were near-drownings—kids who'd been playing on frozen rivers or lakes and had slipped under the water.

Blake Connor, her registrar, looked up from Marcus's arm. 'I've got the bloods.' He rattled off a whole host of tests he planned to run. 'Anything else?'

She shook her head. 'Right now, we're working on the

assumption that he's unconscious due to his hypothermia. There's no sign of any head injury or further trauma. Keep a careful eye on him. I want to know as soon he regains consciousness. He'll probably be disorientated and confused. Most adults with a temperature at this stage start undressing. We might need to sedate him if he becomes agitated.' She scribbled in the notes then spoke to the nursing staff.

'We're aiming for a temperature gain of around one degree every fifteen minutes. Keep an eye on his blood pressure and watch for any atrial fibrillation. Is that clear?'

The nursing staff nodded and she looked around. 'Anyone seen Jackie? She was the one who brought Lily in. I need some more information.'

One of the paramedics touched her arm. 'She fell, coming back up the slope. We think she might have fractured her ankle. Once we'd dropped Lily here my technician took her along to Glasgow Cross.'

Jess felt a twinge of guilt. It was her fault Jackie had been on the scene. She'd wanted the expertise of the experienced nurse at the site. Now, because of her, Jackie was injured. It didn't seem fair.

'Lily's temperature is lower than Marcus's. It's twenty-eight degrees.' Harry had just finished sliding the oesophageal temperature monitor into place. He glanced at the monitor. 'She's borderline, Jess. What do you want to do?'

Jess pulled back the warming blankets to get a better look at her small body. Lily was right on the edge, hovering between severe and moderate hypothermia. It was a wonder she hadn't gone into cardiac arrest.

'How's her respiratory effort?'

Harry was sounding her chest. 'For a child who was submerged I'm not hearing any fluid in her lungs. Just a few crackles. She is breathing, but not enough to keep me happy.'

'Wait a minute, folks.' Jess held her hand up as the monitor flickered, going from a stable but slow heart rate to a run of ectopic beats. She shook her head.

Time was of the essence here. She needed to make a decision.

Lily was deathly pale. All her surface blood vessels had contracted as her little body was focusing its resources on keeping her vital organs warm.

Her lips and ears were tinged with blue, showing lack of oxygen perfusing through her body.

Her eyes fell on Lily's fingers and toes. Their colour was poor.

No. Their colour was worse than poor.

The blueness was worse.

The tinkle of the monitor indicated Lily had gone into cardiac arrest. Jessica leaned across the bed and automatically started cardiac massage with the heel of one hand.

It clarified things and made the decision easier.

'Harry, we're not going to wait. Call the team. Let's get her to Theatre and begin extracorporeal rewarming. Can you phone ahead? Let them know we are resuscitating.'

One of the nurses nodded and picked up the phone in the resus room. 'Paediatric ECMO in Theatre ASAP. Yes, it's one of the minibus victims. Four-year-old female, submerged, with a core temperature of twenty-eight degrees. She's arrested and currently being resuscitated. Dr Shaw has her intubated and they'll be bringing her along now.' She replaced the receiver. 'Theatre one will be waiting for you.'

A wave of relief washed over Jessica. There was no drama. No struggling to find theatre time. It sounded as though the theatre staff was already prepared for the possibility of one of the hypothermic kids needing ECMO.

Extracorporeal membrane oxygenation worked with cardiopulmonary bypass to take over the function of the heart and provide extracorporeal circulation of the blood where it could be rewarmed and oxygenated. It had only been used in a few cases of hypothermia with cardiac arrest in the last few years, but had had extremely positive results with good outcomes for patients.

Lily was going to be one of those patients.

Jessica was absolutely determined.

Two porters appeared at either side of the trolley, ready for the move.

As they swept down the corridor towards the lifts she caught sight of Callum again, taking notes and talking to one of the nurses. He was still here?

She hadn't had a chance to think about him. She had been too busy concentrating her energies on keeping this little girl alive. She could feel the cold flesh under her hand as she pumped methodically, trying to push blood around Lily's body. Trying to get some oxygen circulating to her body and brain.

This was somebody's child. Somebody's pride and joy.

Their reason to get up in the morning and their reason to go home at night.

Any minute now some poor, frantic man and woman would turn up in A and E anxious to get news of their daughter.

Praying and pleading to hear the best possible news. Trying not to think about the pictures their brains had been conjuring up ever since they'd heard about the minibus crash. Struggling to remember to breathe as they made the journey to the hospital.

A journey that probably seemed to take twice as long as it normally did.

Their 'normal' day had changed beyond all recognition. Had they kissed their daughter goodbye that morning before they'd dropped her at nursery? At the place they'd assumed she would be safe?

Had they spent a few brief seconds taking her in their arms and feeling the warmth and joy of cuddling a child before they'd left her that morning? Or had they given her the briefest kiss on the top of her head because they had been in a rush to get to work? Because they hadn't realised it could be the last time they kissed their child.

Would they spend the rest of their lives regretting signing a consent form to say their daughter could go on the nursery trip? The one that could have cost her life?

All these thoughts were crowding her brain. Any time she had to resuscitate a child she was invaded with *what-ifs*?

But the *what-ifs* were about her own life. She'd spent the last three years thinking about the *what-ifs*.

What if she'd been driving the car that night?

What if she hadn't been on call?

What if her husband hadn't stopped to buy her favourite chocolate on the way home?

The lift doors pinged and they swept the trolley out. She lifted her head. The theatre doors were open and waiting for them.

One of the perfusionists was standing by, already scrubbing at the sinks, preparing to insert the catheter lines that could save Lily's life.

This was why she did this job.

This was why after a year of darkness she hadn't walked away. She might not have been able to save her own child but she would do her damnedest to save *this* one.

* * *

Callum stared at his watch. It had been six hours since he'd last seen Jessica sweeping down the corridor, her thin scrub trousers clinging to her wet backside, her hand pumping the little girl's chest.

He'd felt physically sick at that sight.

Not because he wasn't used to dealing with casualties. Casualties of all ages and all descriptions were part and parcel of the job.

But seeing the expression on Jessica's face wasn't.

Everything about this situation was having the strangest effect on him. The sight of Jessica hadn't just been unexpected—it had been like a bolt out of the blue.

They'd been childhood sweethearts who'd broken up when life had moved on and they'd never moved in the same circles again. He hadn't even heard anything about Jessica over the last few years.

Her words on the steep embankment had intrigued him. *Things just didn't work out for me.*

It made his brain buzz. There was a whole world of possibilities in those words. But he didn't feel as if he could come right out and ask.

Particularly when the sick kids were the priority.

And his lasting memories right now were the way her body had felt next to his. The way they'd seemed to fit together so well again—just like they always had.

It was the first time in a long time that he'd felt a connection to a woman.

The first time in a long time he'd ever *wanted* to feel a connection to a woman.

Sure, he'd dated on a few rare occasions, but nothing had been serious. He'd never introduced anyone to Drew. It was almost as if he didn't want to let anyone into that part of his life.

Would he ever feel ready to change that?

The doors opened at the end of the corridor and Jessica walked through. She looked absolutely exhausted. There were black circles under her eyes and her skin was even paler than it had been earlier.

He was on his feet in an instant. 'Jess? How did it go?'

She reached out to touch his arm, her brown eyes fixed on his. 'The next few hours will be crucial. We've done everything we can. Lily's temperature is coming up gradually. Now it's just wait and see. I've just spoken to her parents.' Was that a tear in Jess's eye?

It was there—written all across her face—how much those words pained her. How much she hated it that things were out of her control. The only thing left to do was wait.

She flicked her head from side to side. 'I need to get a report on all of the other kids. I need to find out how they are all doing.'

'No.' He rested his hand on her shoulder. 'You need to take a break. Come and sit down. Have a coffee, have something to eat. You must be running on empty, you know that can't be good for you.'

He could see the struggle in her eyes. 'I just can't, Callum. There were twelve kids in that accident. I'm the consultant on call. They're my responsibility.'

Callum glanced at the notes in his hand. 'Four have already been discharged. Another four have been admitted to the paediatric unit with mild hypothermia, a head injury, and some bumps and scrapes.'

Her eyes widened. 'How do you know all that?'

He gave her a little smile. 'It's part of the investigation after any major incident for the rope rescue crew. I always need to find out the outcomes for the victims. We need to look over everything that we did to make sure there were no mistakes.'

'And were there?'

He frowned. 'Apart from our doctor ending up in the Clyde? And your nurse fracturing her ankle?'

A little smile danced across her weary face. 'I don't think you have much control over tides and currents— no matter how much you want to. And Jackie? That's my responsibility. It was me who asked her to come on the rescue.'

He shook his head. He hadn't been able to shake the picture from his mind of Jessica falling into the icy river. It had made him feel sick to his stomach and would have to form part of his investigation.

'It's my job to make sure everyone is safe at the rescue site. It's my responsibility, not yours.'

Her shoulders relaxed a little. This was probably the first normal conversation she'd had all day. 'Do you want to fight me for it?'

'Will I win?' he quipped.

'Did you ever win?' she quipped back equally quickly.

He smiled. This was the Jess he'd once known.

He glanced at his notes. 'What about the other kids? I know about Marcus and Lily, but that still leaves another two.'

'One was Rosie, she was on the bus next to Marcus. The other is a little girl called Kelly. Both have broken limbs and were taken to surgery by the orthopaedic surgeon.'

'I'll need to follow them up for the report.'

She paused for a second, as if trying to find words. 'It was nice to see you today, Callum, even though it wasn't the best of circumstances. I'm glad you're doing well.'

Something sparked in his brain. She was just about to say goodbye. And he didn't want her to. He didn't want this to be the last time he saw Jessica Rae for another thirteen years.

'But how are you doing, Jess?' The words were out before he had a chance to censor them. Should he really be asking her something like that?

Her eyes lowered, breaking contact with his. Had he offended her? He could see her taking a deep breath.

'If you need any assistance with the investigation, feel free to come back and talk to me.' It was a deliberate side-step. A deliberate attempt to move the conversation back to something more professional.

'I'll need a statement from you about the events.' He would. It wasn't a lie. Any event like this always needed information from all the professionals involved. Not least the one who had landed in the middle of the Clyde.

'That's fine, but can we do it some other time? I really want to check on the kids.'

What she needed to do was to rest. She looked as though a long night's sleep would do her the world of good. But he already knew that wasn't going to happen.

'Of course we can do it some other time. I need to follow up the adults at Glasgow Cross—I'll do that tomorrow. Then I'll come back here to see how the kids are doing.' He hesitated, just for a second. 'Will you be available at any point tomorrow?'

He was hopeful. He was more than hopeful. This might be work, but more than anything right now he'd like to see Jessica again. Any way he could.

She nodded. 'Leave it until later in the day. I'll be busy first thing in the morning with ward rounds and reviews.'

He gave her a little smile and he couldn't help the words that came out of his mouth. 'I'll see you then.'

There was a moment of hesitation, a flicker of something going through her eyes, and it struck straight at his heart. Was it panic? Was it fear?

Her shoulders had pulled back a little, moving away

from him, and the urge to reach out and pull her back towards him raced through his mind.

Why would the simplest of words cause this reaction? Jessica had always been a fun-loving, gregarious young woman. And even though he hadn't seen her in thirteen years this seemed wrong to him. Out of character.

But did he even know Jess's character any more?

It took a few seconds, but Jess seemed to gather herself and gave him the slightest flash of her brown eyes. 'Tomorrow's fine, Callum. I'll see you then.'

She turned and walked down the corridor. He couldn't tear his eyes away from her.

Now, when she was wearing only thin green theatre scrubs, he could see that her weight loss was dramatic. He flinched, remembering having seen the outline of her ribs on the riverbank. Now he could see her legs and hips. Hips that had been pressing up against his earlier.

He'd reached the bottom of the corridor, near the nurses' station in A and E. He recognised one of the sisters— they'd gone to a few study days on some aspects of community safety.

He walked over to her. 'Hi, Miriam, how's things?'

The older woman looked up and shot him a friendly smile. 'Hi, Callum. I take it you were dealing with the kids in the minibus?'

He nodded. 'Not the best day of my life. One of your doctors was out helping us—Jessica Rae?'

Miriam looked confused for a second then waved her hand. 'Oh, you mean Jessica Faraday. I know she's reverted back to her maiden name but I can't get used to it. She's fabulous. One of the best consultants we've got. The kids were certainly in safe hands with her.'

Callum could feel himself furrowing his brow. 'Jessica Faraday? She was married?'

Miriam finished typing something on the computer. 'Yeah.' She was distracted, concentrating on the words in front of her.

'But she's not now?' Callum couldn't help but probe. Curiosity was killing him.

Miriam met his eyes. 'Sadly not.'

*Things just didn't work out for me.*

Jessica's words echoed in his brain. He still didn't know what they meant, and it just didn't seem right to be asking someone else. It didn't matter that Miriam was a colleague—one he'd spoken to on many occasions—he just didn't feel he could ask anything personal about Jess.

It was an invasion of her privacy. He had no right to ask anything about her. It didn't matter that his curiosity was currently burning so fiercely in his stomach it would probably cause an ulcer.

Suddenly he was conscious of what he'd just done. He'd been around hospitals long enough to know that even the simplest and vaguest questions could be entirely misinterpreted.

Miriam had gone back to her paperwork—not in the least interested in why Callum was asking questions about Jessica. Thankfully, she had a hundred other things to worry about. The last thing he needed was rumours starting to spread in a hospital. He didn't want anyone to get the wrong impression.

What was the wrong impression?

He had no idea what he thought about all this.

All he knew for sure was that the haunted look in Jessica's eyes was going to stick in his brain for the rest of the day. And probably most of the night.

This was wrong. He shouldn't be thinking about her at all.

He had Drew to worry about. His little boy was his

entire life and he didn't want anything to get in the way of that. He *wouldn't* let anything get in the way of that.

The custody battle had been fiercely fought, sapping all his energy and strength. And whilst he'd been on dates in the last year or so, no woman had really attracted his attention. No woman had ever been introduced to his son.

And that was way he intended to continue.

He should walk away.

He should run.

But somehow he knew that come tomorrow afternoon he would be right here.

Right here, waiting for Jessica.

# CHAPTER FOUR

CALLUM STARED AT the clock and pulled out his cellphone again. *How is Drew?* he typed.

Drew had been clingy last night. Definitely not normal for him. He hadn't wanted to go to bed and had just said he didn't feel good.

After a day stuck in the freezing-cold Clyde, all Callum had wanted to do was hold him close. So he'd broken all his own rules and let Drew come into bed beside him.

There hadn't seemed to be anything obvious wrong with Drew. His temperature hadn't been raised. He hadn't had a rash. But he'd had a restless night and when he'd stirred his porridge around his plate that morning Callum had looked at the pale little face and had known he couldn't send him to school today.

Thank goodness for good friends. Julie and Blair were always willing to help out any way they could.

His phone buzzed.

*Not eating and a little tired. But managing to watch the TV. Don't worry. Julie.*

Don't worry. Fat chance.

The door next to him opened. Jess. He stood up straight away and walked over to her. 'How are you? Are you okay?' She looked a little better today. There was some colour in her cheeks, her caramel-coloured hair hung in waves around her shoulders and her pink woollen jumper gave the illusion of some curves.

There it was again. The little surge he'd felt yesterday when he'd seen her. That buzz of attraction. He hadn't imagined it. He hadn't imagined it at all.

She gestured down the corridor. 'I'm fine. Honestly. No ill effects.' She gave him a little smile. She was definitely a little more relaxed today but, then, Parkhill was her comfort zone.

'How are the kids?'

Her expression was still serious. 'We've still got two in ITU, both serious but stable. Four were allowed home yesterday, another four were kept for observation overnight but are being discharged today. The last two will be in for a few days, both have different kinds of fractures.'

He gave her a knowing smile. 'Busy day, then?'

She let out a little laugh. 'What? No way. We've only had another thirty admissions on top of the accident yesterday. It's practically been a walk in the park.'

'Thirty? Is there some kind of outbreak?'

She nodded. 'Yip.' She handed over a set of case notes to the secretary next to them. She folded her arms across her chest. 'It's called a Scottish winter.'

'What do you mean?'

She gave a little shrug. 'It's like this every year. Asthma and chest infections flare up and there's always an outbreak of norovirus somewhere. Public health had to recommend closing two nurseries yesterday.' She waved her hand. 'We've got a baby with chickenpox in ITU. Oh, and the usual slips, trips and falls. We're thinking of putting a sign on the door of ward 1C saying *Only people in fibreglass may pass these doors.*'

He couldn't help the smile dancing across his face. 'It's that bad?'

She gave a little sigh. 'It's just how things are. That, and all the parents that come to the desk and give it laldy.'

He smiled. 'Now, there's a word I haven't heard in a while.'

She rolled her eyes. 'It's the most accurate description. I said it the other day to one of the Spanish registrars and he was totally lost. Thing is, it's never the parents with the sickest kids who cause a scene, it's the ones who probably shouldn't even be in an A and E department and don't think they should be waiting.'

'We get our fair share in the fire service too. Last month it was a guy who called 999 every time his house fire alarm went off.'

'Did he have a fire?'

Callum shook his head. 'Nope. He just kept burning his toast and thought we should come out.'

'Thank goodness. I thought it was just us that got the crazies.'

He looked over at her. Although her outward appearance had improved since yesterday, he could still sense the tiredness in her body.

'Are you sure you want to do this today? We can do it some other time if it doesn't suit you.'

She shook her head. 'You're going to need the statement at some point and it's probably best I do it while it's all still fresh in my mind.'

'Have you got time for a coffee?'

She glanced at her watch. 'Actually, I've got a couple of hours.' She looked around her. 'Can we get out of here for a little while? I need to cover for someone tonight so I'll be here until tomorrow.'

He bit his tongue. From the look of her she'd already covered last night too. Did she really need to do it again? The thought of getting her out of this place was very appealing. Maybe some fresh air and a change of scene would lessen the tiredness in her eyes. There was no way he'd say no to her.

'Sure. As long as you don't mind travelling in a fire and rescue vehicle.'

Her eyes widened. 'You've got a fire engine sitting outside?' He could hear the edge of excitement in her voice. It was almost everyone's childhood dream to ride in a fire engine.

He laughed. 'No, I've got the four-by-four. But I'm on call and can be paged at any time, so I need to be ready to go.'

'Oh.' She looked a little disappointed. 'Does that mean you can't go anywhere?'

He shook his head, his heart clenching a little as he realised she'd looked a little sad at the prospect. 'Of course I can. But let's not go too far. That way, if I get paged I can drop you back here quickly. Is there somewhere local you'd prefer?'

She nodded. 'There's an Italian coffee shop that does great food and some killer carrot cake about five minutes' drive from here. Just let me grab my bag and coat.'

He stood for a few seconds until she reappeared at his side, wearing a thick purple wool coat and pink scarf. He smiled. 'I take it you came prepared today.'

'After yesterday? I've honestly never been so cold. The first thing I did last night was put on the fire, find the biggest, snuggliest pair of pyjamas I could and pull my duvet in front of the fire.'

The picture was conjured up in his head instantly. Snuggly pyjamas might not be the sexiest nightwear he would normally think of for a woman, but it still brought a smile to his face.

They walked outside into the cold air and she automatically moved a little closer to him, letting his body shield her from the biting wind. It was all he could do to stop his arm reaching out to wrap around her waist.

He felt on edge. He hadn't seen her in years. She had a whole other life he knew nothing about. Little things started to edge into the corners of his mind. Who did Jessica have to snuggle up to after a stressful day at work? Had she spent the night alone in front of the fire?

Curiosity was killing him. Particularly after the comment Miriam had made the previous day about Jessica reverting to her maiden name.

He had a burning sensation to find out why. It suddenly seemed really important—even though it shouldn't. Did Jessica feel the nervous edge that he did?

But Jess seemed relaxed around him. She shot him another smile as she climbed into the car. 'You would have been horrified. I even resorted to bedsocks last night!'

'Were they pink?' He started the car and pulled out of the car park.

'How did you guess?'

'Because some things don't change.' Pink had always been her favourite colour. The words had come out before he'd had time to think about them. Because nothing could be further from the truth. Things had changed, for both of them—probably more than they could ever have imagined.

Thirteen years was a long time.

There was silence for a few seconds, as if she was thinking the same kind of thoughts that he was.

She gestured to the side. 'This way.' She waited until he changed lanes. 'I guess I always did like pink,' she said quietly. She touched the collar of her coat. 'I've even got a pink coat, I just didn't wear it today.'

Another little memory sparked into his brain. Jessica's wardrobe. She'd had the biggest array of clothes he'd ever seen. He shot her a smile. 'Knowing you, you've probably got a coat for every colour of the rainbow.'

She tilted her head to the side as if she was racking her brain. 'Emerald green.'

He raised his eyebrows.

'That's the colour I'm missing. I need to get an emerald-green raincoat and the rainbow will be complete.' She pointed in front of them. 'It's just over here. Pull in to the left.'

He halted just in front of the Italian-style coffee shop, walking around and opening the door for her.

The heat hit them as soon as they walked inside, along with a whole host of mouth-watering smells.

He pulled out a chair and helped her off with her coat, before sitting across from her and bringing out his array of paperwork. But his brain wasn't focusing on the paperwork.

Taking Jessica out of her own environment felt a little odd. It felt personal but this was business. A professional meeting. Nothing more, nothing less. No matter how casual it seemed.

No matter how *easy* it seemed.

Why did he have to keep reminding himself about that?

He pointed to the menu. 'What do you recommend?'

'Anything and everything. There won't be a single thing in here that you don't like.'

The waitress appeared at their side.

'Just a latte for me, please.'

'No.'

He couldn't help it. Her thin frame was too much for him. He was resisting the temptation to just order her some mushrooms, a portion of lasagne and some garlic bread. Things they used to eat together a long time ago and he knew that she liked.

He couldn't help but wonder who was looking out for Jess right now. Surely her friends had spoken to her quietly and told her she'd lost too much weight? It didn't matter that he hadn't seen her in years, he couldn't stand by and say nothing.

The waitress looked a little taken aback. Callum's eyes ran down the menu. 'You need more than just coffee. Order something else.'

He could see her take a deep breath, getting ready to argue with him. But he shook his head, the smallest of movements, then reached over and touched her hand. 'Don't.'

He kept his gaze steady. They'd been friends for such a long time. It didn't matter that he hadn't seen her in years. It didn't matter that fate had thrown them together. He had no idea what had happened in the last few years for Jess—and she might never tell him. But he could focus on what was in front of him.

The one thing he could do something about.

And she knew him. She knew him well.

She would know that he would never cause a scene, but she would also know that when he was determined, there was no way around him.

Her brown eyes were fixed on where his hand was touching hers. Was she annoyed? Did she think it inappropriate? Because he'd only done what had felt natural—and it didn't feel inappropriate to him.

He could see the long exhalation of breath, the relaxing of her shoulders, then she lifted her long dark eyelashes to meet his gaze.

The long dark eyelashes that used to tickle his cheeks.

The thought came out of nowhere, triggering a whole host of memories in his brain. Now, *they* could be inappropriate.

Jess's fingers moved under his. She looked at the wait-ress. 'What's the soup?'

'Minestrone or tomato and herb, both served with crusty bread.'

Jess pressed her lips together. 'I'll have the minestrone. Please.' She handed the menu over.

'I'll have the same—the soup and a latte.' Something fired in his brain and he remembered what she'd said in the car. 'And carrot cake—for both of us, please.' It wasn't what he would normally eat at this time. The paperwork was still in front of him. But right now it was the least of his concerns.

Would she tell him what had happened to her in the last few years? And, in return, would he be able to tell her about Drew?

He took the bull by the horns. 'You're thin, Jess. A lot thinner than you used to be. I'd rather have bought you a three-course meal than a plate of soup.'

'Who said I was letting you buy it?'

He smiled. There it was. The spark that had seemed missing at times. The spark that took him back thirteen years.

Every now and then it flared, reappearing out of no-where. Then the thin veil would come back down and the Jessica that he had once known would disappear.

He leaned back in the chair. Sparring with Jess now felt as natural as it had years ago. 'Oh, you're letting me. I can assure you of that.'

'Still a stubborn bossy boots, then, Callum?'

'I had a very good teacher,' was his automatic response. But it only took a second to know what he really should do. He stretched across the table and took both her hands in his. 'Actually, I'm still a concerned friend.'

He could sense her pull back a little. See her wariness at his actions.

'We haven't seen each other in years, Callum. We lost touch. You've no idea what's happened in my life and I've no idea what's happened in yours. If that accident hadn't happened yesterday, our paths might never have crossed again.'

'And that would have been a real shame.' He shook his head. 'I'm not glad the accident happened. I'm not glad those kids were injured. But I am glad our paths have crossed again. It's nice to see you.' His voice was low and the words said quietly. He hoped she could see the sincerity in his eyes.

She paused for a moment then said, 'It's nice to see you again too.' She gave him a little smile. 'You always were a pest when it came to food.' She had a glint in her eye, and he could see her visibly relaxing, sinking a little further into her chair and leaning her elbows on the desk so they were closer.

His reaction was entirely natural—he leaned forward too. 'Jessica Rae, I've no idea what you're talking about.'

She raised her eyebrows, her smile spreading across her face. She placed her head on her hands. 'What about the cookie incident, then?'

He stifled a laugh.

The memories came flooding back. A visit to the cinema with Jess asking him to hold her coffee and cookie that he'd bought her while she went and washed her hands. They'd been running late and the film had already started by the time they'd fumbled to their seats. It had taken Jess a few minutes to lift the napkin from her purchase and the scream she'd let out had caused the whole cinema to jump in shock.

'It was only a tiny nibble.' He shrugged his shoulders.

'It was a giant-size bite! And then you let me think that it was the boy behind the counter—you were going to let me go and complain.'

He couldn't stop laughing now, with the still indignant look on her face thirteen years later. 'Just as well the crumbs gave me away, then.'

Jess started to laugh too. Her shoulders shook as she bent forward and then threw her head back. Jess didn't have a delicate, polite laugh. It was loud and wholehearted, as if it came all the way from her toes.

There was something so nice about this. The way her skin glowed and her eyes sparkled when she laughed like that. The ease and familiarity of being with someone you felt comfortable around. Someone you shared a history with. Someone who made you feel as if you could look into their eyes and trust what they said.

Someone who wouldn't run out on you and your child.

Where had that thought come from?

The door to the café opened and a woman and her child bundled in out of the cold. The little boy's nose was glowing red underneath his woolly hat. He looked around the same age as Drew.

Callum pushed all thoughts of Drew's mother out of his head and leaned forward to pass a comment to Jess. But the expression on her face stopped him dead.

She'd gone from hearty laughter to deathly pale—almost as if she'd been caught unawares. He bit his tongue, stopping himself from asking what was wrong.

He had to give her time. He had to give her space. If Jess wanted to tell him something she would.

There was silence for a few seconds as he could see her gathering herself.

She nodded at his paperwork. 'This could take some time. Shouldn't we get started?'

The barriers were going up again. She was closing herself off from him. Going back to business as usual. 'What do you need from me?'

The waitress appeared and put down two bowls of steaming-hot minestrone and a basket of crusty bread. 'I need you to relax for a bit. I want to see you eat. Once you've finished we'll do my paperwork. I need a detailed statement from you.'

He didn't want the veil to come down. Because when it did Jess had the strangest look in her eyes, almost vacant, as if she was removing herself from the situation. It was obvious that she wasn't feeling any of the same strange sensations that he was. His brain was currently mush.

Being around Jess was flaring up too many memories in his mind. Sharing memories with Jess was both warming and setting off alarm bells in his head. He'd been awake most of the night, thinking about all the good times that they'd had together.

He hadn't even told her about Drew yet. And did he want to? He had no idea what he wanted to do about any of this. Could he be friends with Jessica or was it just a recipe for disaster? He'd just have to wait and see.

# CHAPTER FIVE

IT WAS THE middle of the night. The snow had given way to sleet and was currently battering the windows in the old Glasgow hospital.

Whilst the ward was dark, most of the windows were adorned with festive lights. A Santa, a snowman and a reindeer stood out twinkling against the black night sky outside. A tree with multicoloured lights flickered at the end of the ward, and strings of icicles were hanging from most of the windows outside the ward bays.

A few little bodies shifted under the starched white hospital sheets and coloured blankets. Almost everyone was sleeping—unusual for a children's ward—with only a few little murmurs here and there. Alongside most of the beds were chairs and stools with an array of uncomfortable parents trying to catch a few hours' sleep as they watched over their children.

Jessica padded along the ward in her soft-soled shoes. She loved Christmas in the children's ward. Although most people in her circumstances would want to avoid this place, it was actually the one place at this time of year that gave her a little solace.

There were always people worse off than you.

Actually, no there weren't. No parent should outlive their child.

Here, in the ward, she felt safe. Everyone knew what had happened. No one asked awkward questions. If she needed a few moments on her own, she got them.

If she needed to be amongst people and in company, it was here.

If she needed to feel of value, there was no doubt she was needed here. There was always a little one to cuddle. There was always a parent to talk to in the quiet hours of night—to give some kind of explanation, to give some kind of comfort.

Mostly, she just liked to watch the kids sleeping.

There was nothing more comforting than watching a child sleep.

Tonight she was watching Grace Flynn, a seven-year-old with a rare form of aggressive bowel cancer. She'd had her tumours operated on twice.

Grace was a beautiful child. She wanted to be a ballerina, or an air hostess, or a teacher. She changed her mind every day. But she was becoming frailer and frailer with every visit. The chemotherapy and radiotherapy were having ravaging effects on her body. The surgeries were taking their toll. The battle was becoming harder and harder.

So tonight she was taking a little pleasure in watching Grace sleep. Watching the rise and fall of her little chest.

Moments like this always pained her. What was worse? Your child dying suddenly, with no chance to say goodbye, or dying slowly, painfully right before your eyes?

Her brain couldn't even begin to compare those issues. All she knew was that she would do everything in her power to help Grace and her parents.

Hopefully Grace would be able to be discharged home with her family tomorrow and get to spend Christmas at home.

She would love that. She might be the model patient

but she always had a smile on her face when she was discharged home.

Jessica walked down the corridor, watching the twinkling lights on the windows and appreciating the stillness of the ward.

It wasn't always quiet in here. Some nights it went like a fair. Some nights she didn't even see the inside of her on-call room. Then there were other nights like tonight.

She sat down at the nurses' station and tapped a few keys on the computer, bringing up the file of one of the kids admitted earlier. She would never have been able to sleep anyway.

Images of Callum were currently swimming around in her brain.

It was the oddest of feelings.

Because she didn't know how she felt.

For the last few years she'd been sad. She'd worked hard to put one foot in front of the other and try and come out the other side. And now she finally felt as if she'd reached a plateau.

She didn't cry non-stop any more. She didn't spend every day wishing she didn't need to get out of bed. She wasn't insanely jealous of every woman pushing a stroller in the street.

Oh, she still had moments when things crept up on her and caught her unawares. When she needed a few minutes to gather herself or to wipe the stray tear that appeared on her face.

But things had eased. It was still the first thing she thought about every morning and the last thing she thought about at night. But it didn't fill her every waking moment of the day any more. She'd allowed herself to think about other things. To care a little about other things.

And work was her biggest comfort. It helped her tick

along. It gave her a sense of purpose. A little confidence that she did have a life worth living.

Then something like this happened.

A blast from the past, totally unexpected. Totally unprepared for.

Callum was evoking a whole host of memories. Most of which were good. Some of which were distinctly edged with tinges of pink—the way all teenage first-love memories were.

It was a little unsettling. Not just seeing Callum but the whole host of *what-ifs* that had her flooded her mind afterwards—some of which had permeated her dreams.

What if she'd married Callum? What would her life have been like? Would they still have been together after all this time?

She tried to push the thoughts away. It felt disloyal. Disloyal to the memory of her husband, Daniel, and her little boy, Lewis.

Daniel had been the love of her life. She'd been blissfully happy. She'd thought they'd grow old together. She'd *expected* them to grow old together.

But as much as she'd loved Daniel, the loss of Lewis was even worse. As if someone had ripped her heart right out of her chest and squeezed it until every last drop of blood was gone.

The pain had almost killed her.

Maybe that was why her brain was drifting into unchartered territories. If she'd stayed with Callum, Daniel and Lewis would never have featured in her life.

She would never have suffered such torment and hurt at their loss. She wouldn't have found herself wondering if she wanted to go on. To live a life without them.

Maybe Callum was a safe memory.

She opened her eyes, looking around to see if anyone

had noticed her hunched over the keyboard. Two of the nurses were standing at the door of one of the rooms but they hadn't noticed a thing.

Her pager sounded and she was on her feet instantly. ITU. She had three kids in there right now. The baby with chickenpox and Marcus and Lily from the accident. She started saying silent prayers in her head as she walked swiftly down the corridor. She looked around. It was the dead of night and there was no one else about so she took off. Her soft running footsteps echoed up and down the passages of the long building until she reached the doors and squirted her hands with gel before entering.

The doors swung open. The steady whoosh-whoosh of the ventilators was the first thing that she heard whenever she stepped inside. In most instances it was a soothing sound, often not reflecting the serious condition of the patients inside. She took a quick look around the unit. It was brighter than the rest of the hospital, even though some of lights were dimmed.

She recognised a figure next to Lily's bed and walked over quickly. Pauline, the sister in ITU, was great. She'd been there for ten years, had a whole wealth of experience and, more importantly, good instincts. Jessica trusted her judgement, and she also valued her friendship. She'd been a pillar of strength for Jess in the last few years.

'What's up, Pauline?'

Pauline shook her head. 'She's gone from bradycardic and hypothermic to the opposite. Tachycardic and high temp. Isn't it amazing how kids go from one extreme to the other?'

Jessica cast her eyes over the monitor. Thirty-six hours ago Lily had had a heart rate of fifty and now it was one hundred and sixty. 'Darn it. The ECMO should be keeping her heart rate and temperature steady. She must have an infection somewhere. How's her suctioning been?'

Pauline's lips pressed together. She hated it as much as Jess did when kids got sicker. 'She's been suctioned every four hours and there's been no increase in her secretions.'

Jessica rolled her shoulders back, trying to relieve the tension in her neck and shoulders. Everyone knew that ECMO could have complications—bleeding, infections, neurological damage and kidney damage.

Jessica unwound the pink stethoscope from her neck. 'I'll have a little listen to her chest. It was clear earlier and her chest X-ray was fine, but you know how things can change.'

She placed her stethoscope on Lily's little chest and listened for a few seconds then frowned. 'I can hear crackles in her lungs. Can I have her chart? I'll get her started on IV antibiotics right away.' She scribbled on the chart handed to her. 'Are you okay to make these up or do you want me to do it?'

Most of the nurses in ITU had extended roles. The IV antibiotics could be sent up from the hospital pharmacy but that would take time. Time that Lily essentially didn't have. Pauline nodded her head. 'It's fine. I'll do it. It will only take a few minutes.'

Jessica continued to make a few notes. 'I'm asking for another chest X-ray. I want to see if there's any change from this morning. And I'll be about for the next few hours. Let me know if you have any concerns.'

'Not planning on having any sleep tonight, Jess? You know that's not good for you.' There was concern in Pauline's voice. And it was sincere—she always tried to look out for Jess.

Jess just gave her a little smile and kept writing. Sometimes she just liked to keep her head down.

'I meant to ask you, how do you know Callum?'

The question took her by surprise. She felt on guard, even with a woman she'd always trusted. But Pauline's face was open and friendly. 'Callum Kennedy?' she asked.

'Yeah, the fireman—the rope rescue guy. He was on the phone earlier, enquiring after the kids. He knows we can't give him any specific details. He just wanted to check everything was okay. Apparently he was in yesterday too. The staff say he's gorgeous.'

Callum was in here yesterday? Why hadn't she known that? 'What did he say?'

Pauline's eyebrows rose. 'He said you went way back—that you were old friends.'

She was obviously piquing Pauline's interest, and it made her wish she hadn't asked. Jessica felt the colour flare into her cheeks. What on earth was wrong with her? Callum was a good-looking guy and in a gossip hive like a hospital it was obvious people would comment.

Pauline was still talking as she adjusted the controls on Lily's monitors. 'Even David knows him. Says he's played five-a-side football against him. Apparently he's single.' She gave a little laugh. 'He also says the firefighter football team are a bunch of break-your-leg animals. He says he always volunteers to be goalie when they play against them.'

David. The solitary male staff nurse in ITU who was usually the butt of everyone's jokes. Just as well he was fit for it. He always gave as good as he got. And it was good to have a male in a predominantly female environment. Some babies responded better to a male voice—even seemed to be soothed by it.

And he always told any little boy who woke up scared and ventilated in ITU that the same thing had happened to him as a kid.

Some people were just destined to work with children.

Then again, David had just given her a vital piece of information. Callum was single. It seemed ridiculous. He was a gorgeous man, with a good job, and was fun to be around. Women would be beating a path to his door. Why on earth was he single? And, more importantly, why would she care?

'Jess? What's wrong?'

'Nothing. Nothing's wrong.' She could hardly look Pauline in the eye. Pauline was too perceptive by half. Her cheeks were practically bursting. She felt like some crazy teenager again.

'Jess, honey, no one would ever dare say these words to you. But I will because I care about you. Things are looking easier for you, Jess. Your mood has lifted, you don't have quite as many dark circles under your eyes. And once you start eating again…'

'What do you mean, Pauline?'

Pauline bit her lip. 'I mean that if you and Callum have history, *good history*, that might be a good thing.' She hesitated then continued, 'It might be something to embrace instead of run away from.'

'You think I run away from things?'

Pauline reached over and touched her arm. 'I think that you're ready. I think it might be time to start living your life again. I think it might be time to lift your head above the parapet and see what's out there. Whether that's Callum or someone else.' She gave Jess's arm a little squeeze. 'The next step will be hard, Jess. It might be easier if you took it with someone you used to know.'

She looked at Pauline's hand on her arm. The same place that Callum had touched her. The touch that had made every tiny hair on her arm stand on end and little unfamiliar sparks shoot up her arm. It had felt odd.

She wasn't sure how she felt about any of this. She'd spent

a long time with one man and the thought of another—even one who was familiar—was alien to her. There was still that burning edge of disloyalty. Right now she couldn't even consider that Callum could be anything but a friend. No matter how her body reacted to him. It didn't help that her confidence was at an all-time low.

She caught a glimpse of her reflection in one of the windows in ITU. She hardly recognised herself these days. Even she was aware of how thin she was.

She'd once been proud of her figure. She'd liked the glow about her skin. But all that had been lost in the last three years. She barely even looked in a mirror any more. She got her hair cut when it took too long to dry in the mornings. She only put make-up on to stop people commenting on how pale she looked. What man could ever find her attractive now?

'It's only work, Pauline, nothing else.' The sadness in her voice surprised even her. Why were thoughts like this even entering her mind?

'But maybe it could be something else?' Pauline had raised her eyebrows and there was a hopeful tone in her voice.

Everything about this made her uncomfortable.

'If it hadn't been for the accident, our paths would never have crossed again. It's just some crazy coincidence. Callum isn't interested in me.'

'Isn't he? Well, he apparently asked after you while he was in.'

'He did?' She hated the way her heart had given a little jolt at those words.

Pauline finished checking the controls on the ECMO machine and recorded them in the log. 'Yes. He did.' She stared at Jess. 'All I'm saying is there's a world of possibilities out there. Just leave yourself open to a few.' She hung the chart at the end of the bed and moved across to the next patient.

Jessica gazed at her reflection in the glass. A world of possibilities.

How on earth would she cope with those?

# CHAPTER SIX

CALLUM WAS BORED. Bored rigid.

He usually liked coming to study days. There was always something new to learn in his job and some networking to be done. But this guy had been droning on for what seemed like hours. It felt like he was saying the same sentence over and over again. It didn't matter that the clock had only moved on ninety minutes, it felt like groundhog day.

The door at the back of the auditorium opened and he heard a little murmur around him, accompanied by the sound of over a hundred firefighters straightening up all at once. He turned sideways, trying to see what had caused that effect. Had the chief officer just come into the room?

No. It wasn't the chief officer. It was a woman with caramel-coloured hair and a sway to her step. His mouth fell open. Jess?

All of a sudden he was paying attention to what the man at the front of the room was saying. 'Ladies and gentlemen, I'd like you to welcome Dr Jessica Rae. She's a paediatrician at Parkhill, the children's hospital in Glasgow.'

Callum tore his eyes away from Jessica for a moment—something none of the other men in the room were doing—to look at his programme. It had someone else's name on it for the next lecture.

'Dr Rae is filling in for Dr Shepherd, who had an unexpected family emergency today. We're very grateful that she could find the time to step in for us. Dr Rae will be talking to us about paediatric smoke inhalation and immediate treatment.'

Callum watched as Jessica walked to the front of the room. Her hair was shining and resting in curls on her shoulders. And she was dressed cleverly in layers to hide how thin she was, and in bright colours to complement her skin tone.

'Hey, Callum, isn't that the lady doc from the minibus accident?' the firefighter sitting next to him whispered.

'Yes, it is.' He still hadn't taken his eyes from her. She was wearing a bright blue dress that was draped and gathered at the front. She looked good. She had more colour about her face today and was wearing bright lipstick.

'Wow. She looks gorgeous.' He turned and squinted at Callum, in the way only a friend could. 'Didn't you say you knew her from years gone by?'

Callum shifted uncomfortably in his seat. He knew exactly what was going on in Frank's head. 'Yeah. She's an old friend.'

Frank let out the lowest of whistles. 'Wish my old friends looked like that.'

The hackles at the back of Callum's neck immediately rose. Frank was only voicing what every appreciative man in the room was thinking. But that didn't mean that he liked it. He wanted to put a cocoon around Jess and protect her. Hide her away from the leering glances.

He hadn't seen her in more than a week and, boy, was she a sight for sore eyes. The fact that thought had sprung into his mind alarmed him. Why, all of a sudden, was he annoyed by the fact that other men found her attractive? What right did he have to feel like that?

More than once this week his hand had hovered over the phone, thinking of a reason to phone Jess again. Looking for any excuse just to speak to her.

But then his rational side had kicked in and brought him back into reality.

Too bad reality was looking kind of blurry right now.

Jess stood up at the podium and looked around the room. When her eyes rested on Callum he saw her give a little start, before she gave him a nervous smile.

'Hi, folks. I recognise some of the faces in here today because unfortunately, in our lines of business, our paths frequently cross.' She pressed a button and the presentation appeared on the wall behind her. 'I'm going to give you some up-to-date information on the best things you can do for a child with smoke inhalation.' She lifted her hand and gestured around the auditorium. 'I'm sure it's something you've all had to deal with.'

Jessica was confident at work. She was in control. That much was clearly evident. She could probably have done this presentation with her eyes shut. And it was nice to see her that way.

Her voice was steady and clear. 'We don't expect any of you to do anything more than the most basic first aid. I'm sure you're all aware that the paramedics and ambulances aren't always on scene immediately, so my job today is to give you enough information to feel confident in your first responses.'

She lifted her hand, pressed a button on the remote and the screen behind her changed. Then she turned back and gave the room a dazzling smile. 'Now, let's begin.'

It was officially the quickest thirty minutes of her life. She hadn't hesitated that morning when a colleague had asked her to cover for him. As a paediatric consultant at a teaching hospital she was often asked to give lectures to medical students and people in other disciplines. This was a walk in the park for her.

If only there wasn't a great big distraction right in the middle of the room.

Callum was definitely the proverbial elephant in the room today.

She spent the whole thirty minutes trying to avoid looking at him. She was sure that if she caught a glimpse of his green eyes she wouldn't be able to concentrate at all.

It was strange. She should have felt happy that there was a friend in the room, but instead she felt almost like a student undergoing an examination. It was just as well the firefighters went easy on her and there were only a few questions at the end. That was the beauty of talking just before the coffee break—no one wanted to hang around for long.

As soon as she'd finished the room emptied quickly. Her heart started to thud. Would Callum leave without speaking to her? Maybe he had to network with some of his colleagues and wouldn't have time.

'Hey, Jess. That was a nice surprise.' She started at his voice and turned around quickly as someone jostled him from behind and pushed them even closer together. It looked as if it was a stampede towards the strong smell of coffee.

Her hand went up automatically and rested on his chest. She could feel the heat of his body through his thin black shirt. 'Hey, you too. I didn't expect to be here. Just filling in for a friend.'

'What happened?'

'Mark Shepherd's wife has cancer. She had a bad reaction to her chemo, so he wanted to stay home with her.'

'I'm sorry to hear that. How are the kids from the accident doing?'

She raised her eyebrows. 'You mean you haven't already phoned today?'

He squirmed. 'Okay, I admit it. I'm a bit of a stalker.'

She laid her hand on his arm. 'But only in a good way. We've got four still in, but they're all improving. With kids we just take things one day at a time.'

Callum nodded slowly. He held his elbow out towards her. 'Have you time for some refreshments before you leave?'

'Hmm, firefighter coffee. Is it as bad as I think it will be?'

'Scandalous! We're very serious about our coffee, and we're even more serious about our cakes. I can guarantee you a fruit scone.'

'Something does smell pretty good around here.' She put her hand through his crooked elbow. 'Why do I get the impression that you're trying to fatten me up, Callum?'

He rolled his eyes and pressed his other hand to his chest. 'Tragedy, you've caught me out.' His face broke into a wide grin. 'Let's call it *looking out for a friend.*'

Her heart gave a little flutter. 'Friends? Is that what we are again, Callum?'

'I certainly hope so.' There was something so nice about the way he'd said those words. Not a moment's hesitation. He didn't even need to think about it for a second.

Friends. She liked that word. It felt safe.

They walked across the corridor to the coffee room. The queue had died down a little and she had a little time to peruse the cakes in the glass cabinet. The firefighters certainly did take their coffee seriously. This was an outlet of a popular coffee house, with all their famous tempting products on display.

He placed his arm on the counter and slid a tray in front of her. 'What can I tempt you with?'

Now, there was a question.

The thoughts that flooded her mind almost made her blush.

'I'll have a light caramel latte with two shots and a piece of the banana and nut loaf, please.' The words were automatic. She was used to ordering in one of these coffee shops—she didn't need to think twice.

He seemed pleased. Pleased that she didn't spend forever fretting over what to eat and drink. Patience had never been Callum's strong point.

They waited a few minutes while the barista made their coffee. 'How did you manage to wangle a franchise in here?' she said. 'I didn't think it would be allowed.'

He pointed to a sign near the door. 'Neither did we, but the coffee was getting worse and worse and tempers were fraying. They asked what we wanted and we told them. The profits from this franchise don't go back into the overall company. We have a ballot every year to decide which charity to support.'

He gave a little shrug. 'It works in our favour and in theirs. We get to support the charity of our choice, and they get to put us on their website talking about their contributions to charity. It's good publicity for them.' She smiled at the poster supporting research into Alzheimer's disease. 'Why did you pick that one?'

He picked up the tray and carried it over to a vacant table. 'We get lots of accidental house fires started by older people with memory problems—putting things in the oven or on the hob and forgetting about them. Some have early signs of Alzheimer's. We often go out and do community safety visits and fit fire alarms for anyone referred to us. It seemed a natural pick.' His voice lowered and she could sense the sadness in it. 'It caused us three fatalities last year.'

They sat down and Jess sipped her coffee. It was just as good as it was in every shop in the country. 'I think it's a great idea. I wonder if the hospital would consider it? The hospital kitchens are great, but the staff canteen is run by an outside firm. It's nowhere near as good as this.'

'I can give you some details if you want.'

'That would be perfect.' She leaned back in her chair. 'You could quickly make me the most popular woman in the hospital.'

'I'm sure you're that already.' His voice was low and he was looking up at her from over the top of his steaming cup of coffee.

She couldn't help the little upturn at the corners of her lips. When had the last time been that she'd had a man flatter her? It had been so long ago she couldn't remember.

Sure, there had been the odd unwanted leering comment, the kind that made your stomach turn—and not in a good way.

But this was different. It hadn't been invited. Or expected.

It was just—well, a nice comment. The kind that sent a little rosy glow all through you. Something she hadn't felt in a very long time.

It was kind of weird how she felt about all this. That first glimpse of Callum on the riverbank had been a total shock. And the way her body had reacted—her *natural* instinct—had been even more of a shock.

Because her natural instinctive response to Callum had been very physical. It hadn't helped that they'd been thrust together—in more ways than one—and parts of her body that had seemed dead had suddenly sparked into life.

It was taking time to get her head around all this.

And, to be frank, she was struggling.

In a way she wished she could be that naïve seventeen-year-old again, thinking that her heart was breaking as she left her first love behind.

If only she'd known then what she knew now.

That wasn't the thing that broke your heart. Not even close.

But all her memories of Callum were good. They were safe. Even if they came with a heavy dose of passion and teenage angst.

She didn't feel afraid around Callum. And she liked the way he was looking at her. It made her feel as if she was finally worth looking at again.

Pauline's words echoed around her head. *A world of possibilities.*

'Callum, I need to speak to you about something.'

The words jerked Jess out of her daydream. A well-stacked blonde was directly in her line of vision, her boobs inches from Callum's nose. Were those real?

'We need to talk about the meeting tomorrow at city headquarters. I need to give you a report to review before you go.'

Strange things were happening to Jess. The hackles had just gone up at the back of her neck and she felt an intense dislike for this extremely pretty and apparently efficient blonde. What on earth was wrong with her? She was never like this.

'Hi, Lynn. I'm actually in the middle of something right now.'

'What?' She glanced over at Jessica—whom she'd completely ignored—with renewed interest. 'Well, I'll let you finish up. But I'll need to see you in five.'

She turned to sweep away. Jess felt a smile sneak across

her face as she realised Callum hadn't stared once at the boobs on display.

'Actually, I'll be a bit longer than that.' He gave a wave of his hand. 'I'll come and find you later.'

Lynn shot him a look of surprise, but Callum wasn't even looking at her any more. His attention was completely on Jessica.

Jess's heart gave a little flutter. She'd just recognised the sensation she'd felt a few seconds ago on Lynn's approach. Jealousy.

It was almost as if she'd landed in the middle of the icy-cold Clyde again, with the freezing water sweeping over her skin.

There was something very strange about all this. Being around Callum was making her feel again, something she thought would never happen. She'd been switched off for so long that she wasn't recognising everything straight away.

This was dangerous territory. She would have to take baby steps.

But all of a sudden it didn't seem quite so scary.

She gave Callum a little smile. 'So, tell me more about uni.'

She had to start somewhere and it was as good a place as any.


'Daddy, I don't feel good.'

Callum was sleeping but the little voice jerked him straight out of the weird dream that was circulating around his brain. Jessica dressed in a clown suit. Where did these things come from?

Yesterday had been fun. They'd spent most of the time together reminiscing. Talking about their past seemed to relax Jess. And he liked her like that.

He also liked the fact he was spending time with someone he trusted. Someone he didn't need to feel wary around. Somebody who wouldn't let him down.

But right now his paternal radar was instantly on alert. Drew was standing in the doorway, his eyes heavy with sleep and his hand rubbing his stomach. This was the second day he hadn't felt great. The second night Callum had put his dinner untouched into the bin.

Over the last two weeks Drew's symptoms seemed to flare up and then die down again.

He lifted up the corner of his duvet. 'Come over here so I can see you.'

Drew scuttled across the room and straight under the cover next to his dad. Callum pressed his hand to his head. He didn't feel warm—no obvious temperature. 'What's wrong, big guy? Do you feel sick?'

According to Drew's primary teacher half the class were off with a sickness bug. Maybe some of them had even ended up in Jessica's hospital. Rumours were circulating that it was norovirus.

Just what he needed. He still had the accident report to complete and there had been another incident at work today that would need to be followed up.

'Not sick, Daddy. Just a rumbly tummy.'

'Are you hungry? Is your tummy rumbling because you didn't eat any dinner?' He glanced at the clock. Two a.m. 'Do you want Dad to make you some toast?' It wasn't an ideal situation but if it settled Drew and got him back to sleep quickly, he could live with it.

Drew lay back against the pillows. 'No. Not hungry.' He moved a little closer. 'Just rub my tummy, Daddy, that will make it better.'

'You're sure? Do want a little drink of water?'

Drew shook his head and closed his heavy eyes.

Callum's hand automatically moved into position, very gently rubbing Drew's tummy in little circles. What could be wrong?

He hated to overreact. He hated to be an over-anxious father. But the truth was he had very few people he could bounce things like this off.

His friends Julie and Blair were the obvious choice but he wasn't going to call them at this time of night.

He glanced at the clock again. Maybe he would take Drew back to the GP in the morning. The trouble was, he hated going to the GP with a list of vague symptoms. A list of *not much but maybe it could be.*

It made him feel paranoid. It made him feel as if he wasn't coping. And that was the last thing he wanted anyone to think.

Did single mothers feel like this too?

Drew was the most precious thing in the world to him. He couldn't live with himself if he brushed something off and it turned out to be serious.

Maybe he should have asked Jessica yesterday. She was a paediatrician, she knew everything there was to know about kids.

But he hadn't thought about it and that made him feel a little guilty. He hadn't even told her about Drew yet. Should he have? Theirs was a professional relationship. Nothing more, nothing less. But a tiny little part of his brain was nagging away at him, thinking that maybe it could be something else.

He still hadn't got to the bottom of her words. *Things just didn't work out for me.*

She'd been really careful today to keep steering the conversation back to him—or work, whenever he'd asked anything vaguely personal. She'd mentioned her mum and dad, a few old friends they'd known years ago. But nothing about herself.

Maybe he should wait until he found out what that meant before he gave it another thought.

He cuddled up with his little boy. Drew was his top priority right now.

The first person he looked at in the morning and the last person he looked at at night.

And that's the way it would stay.

## CHAPTER SEVEN

THE WARD WAS quiet and he'd no idea where Jessica was. The nurse had just pointed down in this general direction.

He walked past a few windows, seeing children lying in beds with anxious parents next to them.

His heart clenched slightly. He would hate to be in that position. Thank goodness Drew usually kept in good health. He still hadn't got to the bottom of that stomach ache. The GP had basically fobbed him off and Callum didn't blame him because when they'd finally got an appointment, Drew had been full of beans and jumping around the place.

It was always the same with kids.

The ward sister he'd met a few times was standing next to one of the doors. 'Hi, Pauline.'

She gave him a knowing smile. 'Hi, there, Callum. And who might you be looking for?'

He sighed. He'd known from the first time he'd met her that Pauline could read everyone instantly. Why even pretend it was anything else? He still hadn't seen Jess, so this might work in his favour.

He leaned against the doorjamb and folded his arms. 'Let's just say I'm looking for our favourite doc.' He lifted his eyebrows. 'All work-related, of course.'

Pauline nodded. 'Of course.' But the smile was spreading further across her face. She lowered her voice. 'I think our mutual friend will be very pleased to see you.'

He felt something flare inside him. That acknowledgement—no matter how brief—reassured him. Pauline and Jess were good friends. If Jess was talking to anyone it would be Pauline. It gave him a little hope. It also gave him the courage to ask the question that had been gnawing away at him.

He hesitated for a second. 'Pauline—about Jess.'

She raised her eyebrows, as if he was about to say something she didn't want to hear. She was protective of Jess and that was nice.

'Jess told me that things didn't work out for her. And I know she's reverted to her maiden name.' He unfolded his arms and held out his hand towards her. 'I wonder if you could tell me what happened. I get the feeling I'm treading on difficult ground.'

Pauline bit her lip and glanced over her shoulder. Her eyes met his. 'You're right, Callum, it is difficult ground but I think that it's something Jess really needs to tell you herself.' Her eyes looked down, as if she was hesitant to say any more. 'Life hasn't turned out the way she expected. Jess should be married with a family to love and I'm hoping that's what she'll get. Just give her a little time.'

She pointed to the next set of doors. 'She's down there. Go and say hello.'

Was this better or worse?

His curiosity had just scaled up about ten notches.

He wanted to give Jess time to tell him—he really did. There was just that little edge of wariness. That lingering feeling left by a previous experience.

Jess was nothing like Kirsten, Drew's mother. They weren't even in the same ballpark. But it didn't stop his slightest sense of unease as he walked down the corridor.

He pushed the feelings to one side. He'd already made up his mind about what he wanted to do next. He wanted to see how Jess would react. And he wouldn't know unless he tried.

Finally he caught sight of Jess's caramel-coloured hair. She was sitting talking to a little girl with curly hair with her leg in a bright pink fibreglass cast. It was Rosie, from the minibus accident.

He stuck his head around the door. 'Knock, knock.'

Jess looked surprised to see him. 'Callum, what are you doing here?'

'I phoned and left you a message. Didn't you get it?'

She shook her head then turned to the woman sitting next to her. 'Carol, this is Callum Ferguson. He's one of the fire rescue crew who were at the accident. He helped get Rosie out of the bus.'

'It's him, Mummy! It's him!' Having a cast on hadn't seemed to limit Rosie's movements. She wiggled over to the edge of the bed. 'The one I told you about.'

Rosie's mum stood up and held out her hand. 'Callum, my daughter has been talking about you non-stop. She seems to think you're a superhero. She saw you abseil down the side of the riverbank.'

Callum felt a little rush of blood to his cheeks. This was the last thing he had been expecting. He shook his head and knelt down beside the bed. 'You're much braver than me, Rosie. You tumbled down the bank in the minibus. That must have been really scary. The way I got down wasn't scary at all.'

Rosie held out her hands and reached round Callum's neck, giving him a big hug.

Jessica was watching. Watching—and trying to keep the smile from her face at his appearance. Callum seemed totally at ease, not in the least fazed by the little girl's action. Thank goodness. She had him on some sort of pedestal.

But it was kind of nice. Almost as if he was used to being in contact with kids.

Callum leaned back and tapped the pink cast. 'How is your leg? I love the colour of your cast.'

Rosie smiled. 'Thank you. Dr Rae and I have the same favourite colour. That's why I picked pink.'

'Well, I think it looks great. Your leg will be all better soon.'

Jess stood up and gave Carol and Rosie a smile. 'I'll leave you two. You can give me a call if you need me.' She nodded her head towards the door. 'Callum?'

She could smell his aftershave. It wasn't familiar. It was different from the one he'd used the day they'd abseiled back up the slope. It was more spicy, with richer tones. She liked it.

They walked along the corridor. Callum waved his hand, in which he had a big brown envelope. 'I've typed up the statement from the other day. I need you to read over it and sign it.'

She felt a flutter of disappointment. Business. Purely business. That's why Callum was here. Not for any other reason. A strange lump was forming in her throat. Once she'd signed the statement she would have no reason to ever see Callum again.

Her heart had leapt when he'd appeared. She hated it when it did that. She kept telling herself over and over again that this was nothing. This meant nothing. Just some wild, crazy coincidence that their paths had crossed again. This was work-related.

He turned to face her and she tried hard not to stare at his chest, which was instantly in her view.

She raised her eyes to meet his bright green ones. It was

one of the first things she'd ever noticed about Callum, his startling green eyes.

'I can read the statement now, it will only take a couple of minutes.' There was no point turning this into something it wasn't. She saw him glancing at his watch, it was nearly six o'clock in the evening. He would be finished for the day—just the way she should be. Was he worried about being late? Did he have a date? Maybe that blonde from the fire station?

She hated the way that thought made her stomach curl.

'Have you finished for the day?'

'What?'

He'd moved a little closer and was towering over her, an impatient edge to his voice.

'I mean have you finished? You can't be on call again. I want you to come somewhere with me.'

She pulled back a little. There was something a little weird about him. Was he nervous?

She looked around her. The ward had quietened down. All patients had been seen, all prescriptions and instructions written. 'Yes, yes, I'm finished.' She was feeling a bit bewildered. A few seconds ago she had been sure everything was business as usual. He needed a signature to get the job finished so he could be on his way. And that had made her sad.

Now what?

A smile broke across Callum's face. 'Then get your coat.' She was turning towards her office when she heard him mutter something under his breath. 'You've pulled.'

She let out a burst of laughter and spun back around. 'Did you just say what I think you did?'

It had been a joke between them. A daft teenage saying that both had used years before. But it came totally out of the blue and instantly took her back thirteen years.

Callum's shoulders were shaking. 'Sorry, I couldn't resist it.'

Jessica stuck her hand around the office door and pulled out her woollen coat. There was a flash of bright pink. 'Think you can cope?' she asked as she wound her purple scarf around her neck and fastened the buttons on the bright coat.

He just nodded. 'You did warn me about the bright pink coat, and knowing you I wouldn't have expected anything less. Do you have gloves?'

She stuck her hands in the coat pocket and pulled out a pair of purple leather gloves. 'Sure. Why?'

'It's a nice night out there. Just a little dusting of snow. I'd like to walk instead of drive. Are you okay with that?'

She pulled out a woolly hat and stuck it on her head. 'I'm game if you are. But you've got me curious now. Where are we going?'

He gestured towards the door. 'Let's find out.'

They walked quickly through the lightly falling snow. It was pitch dark already—darkness fell quickly in winter in Scotland. The streetlights cast a bright orange glow across the wet pavements.

'So where are you taking me?'

Callum drew in a breath. He was still getting over the fact he'd asked her. It had been totally instinctive. He'd only made the decision once he'd set foot on the ward—particularly after what Pauline had said to him. The words had come out before he'd even had a chance to think about them. A signature would have meant he'd have no excuse to see Jesssica again. And he wasn't quite ready for that.

Drew was at mini-kicker football tonight. He went every week with Julie and Blair's son. One week Callum gave them dinner and took them, the next week Julie and Blair took them. Drew wouldn't be home until after eight o'clock.

'That would be a surprise.'

'Hmm…a surprise. How do you know I still like surprises?'

He gave her a little smile. 'It's an educated guess. Some things are just part of us—like our DNA. I'm working on the premise that the fundamentals haven't changed.'

They turned a corner and started walking along one of the main roads. It was busier now, the crowds jostling along all seeming to be headed in one direction.

The strains of Christmas music could be heard above the buzz of the crowds around them. Jess stopped a few times to look at the Christmas displays in some of the shop windows. Finally, he placed his hand in the small of her back as he guided her around the corner and into George Square.

'Oh.' He heard the little bit of shock in her voice as the recognition of where they were sank in. The square was bustling, packed with people here to see the annual switching on of the Christmas lights. A huge tree stood in the middle of the square, already decorated and just waiting for the lights to be lit. The Lord Provost already stood on the stage, talking into a microphone and trying to entertain the crowds.

'You brought me here? I can't believe you remembered.' Her voice had gone quiet, almost whispered.

This had been one of their first dates, coming to see the annual switching on of the Christmas lights in George Square. He hadn't planned this. He hadn't even thought about it. But as he'd driven to the hospital tonight he'd heard the announcement on the radio about the switch-on. It had almost seemed like a sign—a message. He'd had to

ask her to come along. If only to try and take a little of the
sadness out of her eyes.

'There's so many families,' she said as she looked
around, dodging out of the way of a little girl with long
blonde hair running straight for them.

'Yeah, there always are.' Lots of people brought their
families to the turning on of the lights. It was entirely normal. But he couldn't help catch the little edge of something
else in her voice.

'Over here.' Callum put his hand on her back again
and guided her over to one of the street-vendor stalls. The
smells of cloves, mulled wine and roasted chestnuts were
all around them. Callum bought two cups and handed one
over to her.

'Want to take a guess at what colour the tree lights will
be this year?'

Jessica leaned against one of the barriers, sipping her
mulled wine and watching the people around them. It was
obvious that her brain was trying to take in their surround-
ings. 'They were purple the first year that we came here.'

'And they were silver the year after.' He kept his voice
steady.

'And red the year after that.'

It was clear that they both remembered and for some
reason it was really important to him that it was imprinted
on Jess's brain just as much as it was on his. Half of him
had been sure she would know why he'd brought her here,
while the other half had been in a mad panic in case she'd
turned around with a blank expression on her face.

'They were blue last year,' he murmured, not really
thinking.

Jess spun round, the mulled wine sloshing wildly in her
cup. 'You were here last year?'

Yes. He'd been here with Drew. But it had turned out

Drew didn't really like the turning on of the lights. It was almost as if there was a little flare of panic in Jess's eyes. Did she think he'd been here with another woman?

Maybe this was it. Maybe this was time to tell her about Drew. It seemed natural. It was a reasonable explanation for what he'd just said. But the look in her eyes, that and the wistful tone in her voice when she'd remarked on the families, made him think twice.

'I was here with some friends.'

'Oh.' She seemed satisfied with that answer and rested her forearms back on the barrier.

The crowd thickened around them, pushing them a little closer together as people jostled to get a better place at the barrier. Callum wound his arm around her waist, holding her firmly against him, to stop anyone coming between them. The countdown around them started. Ten, nine…

It was the smallest of movements. Jess rested her head on his shoulder then a few seconds later he felt her relax a little more and felt some of the weight of her body lean against him.

A grin spread across his face. It wasn't like anyone could see it but it had been automatic and was plastered there for the world to see. Three, two, one.

'Woah!' The noise went around the crowd as the lights flickered on the tree, lighting up the square in a deluge of pink and silver.

'Pink! It's pink!' Jess yelped, as the wine sloshed out of the cup and she turned to face him. Her eyes were sparkling, her excitement evident. It was the first time since he'd seen her again that she looked totally carefree. Totally back to normal.

Her face was right in front of his, her brown eyes darker than ever before and their noses almost touching. He could see the steam from her breath in the cold night air. He placed his cup on the barrier and brought his hand to her hip, matching the hold of his other hand, and pulled her a little closer. He gave her a smile.

'My plan worked. I told them that pink was your favourite colour and that you'd be here.'

She let out a laugh and placed her hands on his shoulders. She didn't seem annoyed by him holding her. She didn't seem annoyed at all. In fact, if he wasn't mistaken, she was edging even closer.

Her dark eyes were still sparkling, reflecting the twinkling lights around them, 'Oh, you did, did you? I bet that took a bit of planning, especially as you didn't even know if I'd agree to come on a walk with you.'

He pulled her even closer. 'Oh, I knew. I was absolutely sure you'd come with me.'

He could turn back the clock. He could flick a little switch right now and this could be thirteen years ago. Standing almost in this exact spot.

She tilted her head to the side. 'Well, that was a bit presumptuous, wasn't it?'

He shook his head. 'I don't think so. But this might be.'

He bent forward. People around them were still cheering about the Christmas lights, breaking into song as the music got louder in the amplifiers next to them.

But Callum wasn't noticing any of that. The only thing he was focused on was Jess's lips.

And everything was just like he remembered. Almost as perfect.

The last time round Jess had tasted of strawberry lip gloss, and this time she tasted of mulled wine. He could sense the tiniest bit of hesitation as he kissed her, so he took it slowly, gently kissing her lips, teasing at the edges until she moved her hands from his shoulders and wrapped them around his neck, kissing him right back.

And then everything *was* perfect.

# CHAPTER EIGHT

CALLUM LISTENED TO the NHS helpline music with growing impatience. It was funny how all rational thought flew out of the window when your child was in pain.

Drew was clutching his stomach again. He was pale and feverish, and he couldn't even tolerate fluids. But the pain was making him gasp and sob and Callum was feeling utterly helpless.

He glanced at his watch. It would be nearly midnight by the time the NHS helpline put him through to one of the nurses—and he told Drew's story *again*—then they would have to drive out to one of the GP centres. Who knew when his son would get some pain relief?

No. He couldn't wait that long.

As a member of one of the emergency services, he hated it when people used the services irresponsibly. But this didn't feel irresponsible. This did feel like an emergency. And he could explain later why he hadn't been prepared to wait for the helpline.

Jessica was on call tonight. Should he take Drew to Parkhill?

He hadn't even told her about Drew yet, and this would be a baptism of fire. But as Drew's father he couldn't think of anyone he would trust more with his son. He'd seen Jessica at work. He'd heard her colleagues talk about her.

She was undoubtedly a great doctor, who cared about her patients.

He was supposed to be taking Jessica out for dinner in a few nights' time. He'd been hoping to tell her about Drew then, and also to explain why evening dates could prove to be difficult. After a day of work he really didn't like to ask someone to babysit his son. He wanted to spend time with him. And he was hopeful that Jess would understand that. But now that would all have to wait.

Within minutes he had Drew bundled up into his booster seat, still in his pyjamas and wrapped in a fleecy blanket.

The roads were coated with snow and deadly quiet. Anyone with a half a brain was tucked up in bed. The only other traffic on the roads at this time of night was the gritters. He made it to the hospital in record time, parked in one of the emergency bays and carried Drew inside in his arms.

'I need to see Jessica Rae right away.'

The receptionist looked up, her face unfamiliar. 'Can you give me your details, please, sir?'

'Jessica Rae—I know she's on duty tonight. I want her to check over my son.'

The receptionist plastered a weary smile on her face. 'Give me your son's details. I'll get one of the doctors to see him.'

Callum felt his patience at an all-time low. 'Page Jessica Rae for me—*now*!'

One of the triage nurses appeared at his side and gave a knowing smile to the receptionist. They were probably used to frantic parents, but it didn't excuse his behaviour. 'Come with me, sir, and I'll start the assessment procedure for your son.' She reached over and brushed Drew's fringe out of his eyes, taking in his pale colour and the sheen on his skin. 'Let's get some obs.'

Callum felt himself take some deep breaths as he followed the nurse down the corridor. She was ruthlessly
efficient, taking Drew's temperature, heart rate and blood
pressure, then putting some cream on the inside of one
elbow to numb the area and prepare it for a blood sample
to be taken. As she scribbled down Drew's history, then
held a sick bowl to let him retch into it, she gave Callum
a tight smile.

'I know you asked for Dr Rae, but she's in surgery right
now. She will see your son, but he needs some other tests
done and some blood taken in the meantime. I'm going to
ask one of the other doctors on duty to see Drew right now.'

There was something in the way she said the words. The
quiet urgency in them. As if she suspected something but
wasn't prepared to say it out loud. She had that look about
her—the nurse who'd seen everything a dozen times and
could probably out-diagnose most of the junior doctors.

'What do you think's wrong?'

She gave the slightest shake of her head. 'Let's leave
that to the doctors, shall we?'

He tried his best not to erupt. To tell her that he didn't
want his son to wait a second longer.

She glanced at him as she headed to the curtains. 'I'll
get the other doctor now. The sooner Drew is seen, the
better. Then we can get him some pain relief.'

He nodded automatically. Pain relief for his son. That's
what he wanted more than anything. Anything to take the
pain away from Drew.

'Dr Rae, there's a kid with an acute abdomen in A and E.
Father is insisting you see him.'

Jessica pulled off her gown and gloves and dumped
them in the disposal unit. 'Really? What's the name?'

'Kennedy. Drew Kennedy.'

She shrugged. She was the consultant on call. She'd see any kid with an acute abdomen anyway. 'I don't recognise the name, but tell them I'll be right there.'

She gave her hands a quick wash, trying to place the name. None of her friends had a son called Drew. And the surname? Well, there was only one Kennedy that she knew.

Her stomach gave a little sinking feeling as she rounded the corner into A and E. It couldn't be, could it?

No. Not a chance.

It couldn't be a nephew as Callum didn't have any brothers or sisters.

And Callum would have mentioned something as important as having a son. Wouldn't he?

But as she walked over to the curtains she recognised the frame hunched over the little figure straight away.

She froze.

She wanted to turn on her heel and run away. She wanted to disappear out of the hospital and take a minute to catch her breath. To try and get her head around the thousand thoughts currently spinning around in her brain.

But that was the second that Callum looked up. And his relief at seeing her was plastered all over his face.

She'd seen that look a hundred times. The parent worried out of their mind about their child. Hoping against hope that their worst fears weren't about to be realised.

Professional mode. No matter how she felt, or what her questions were, she had to move into professional mode right now. There was a sick little boy to be dealt with.

She kept her voice steady and calm. 'Callum? I didn't expect to see you.' She picked up the chart, her eyes skimming over the notes and observations. 'Is this your son?'

Calm. Rational. That's how she was hoping she sounded.

Callum had the good grace to look embarrassed. 'Yes. This is Drew.' There was a shake to his voice. He really was scared for his son—he must be. He'd deliberately brought him here and asked for her, even though he'd known she would have questions. 'He's five and he's had a sore stomach on and off for the last two weeks. We've been back and forth to the GP with no diagnosis. But tonight he's much worse.' He lowered his voice. 'Sorry. I was going to tell you about Drew at dinner on Saturday.'

Her brain was still stuck on the 'five' part. She tried not to wince as she glanced at the date of birth. Drew was almost the same age as her son Lewis would have been.

She tried not to let the tight squeeze around her heart affect her. Everything was so unfair. Callum had the little boy she should still have. A little boy he hadn't even mentioned.

She took a deep breath and looked over at the little boy on the bed. The junior doctor had done everything he should, but he hadn't made any provisional diagnosis. Which meant he was stumped.

'Hi, there, Drew. I'm Dr Jessica. Do you mind if I have a look at your tummy?'

'No. Daddy, don't let them touch my tummy again.' She could hear the distress in the little boy's voice. The fear of someone touching a part of him that was already very painful.

She looked at the chart, making sure he'd been given some analgesia. 'Hasn't the medicine helped your sore tummy? It should have made it feel a little better.'

The little boy shook his head. 'It's still sore.'

'Can you tell me where it hurts if I promise not to touch?'

He nodded. His face was pale. 'It started in the middle but now it's over here.' He pointed to his left side.

She pointed to the IV in his arm. 'I'm going to put a little more medicine in here. It will work really quickly and help your tummy.' She nodded towards the nurse. 'Can I have point two milligrams of morphine, please?'

She waited a few minutes until the nurse returned with the syringe and ampule for her to check before administration. She prescribed the dose and signed the ledger before giving Drew the analgesic. She placed her hand on his forehead and bent down to whisper in his ear, 'It will start to work really quickly, I promise.'

Some doctors didn't agree with giving analgesia to paediatric patients before a diagnosis was made. They thought it could mask abdominal symptoms and delay a diagnosis. But Jessica had read a whole host of studies with evidence that analgesics reduced pain without interfering with diagnostic accuracy. Besides, Jessica could never leave a child in pain.

Right now, Drew was showing most of the signs and symptoms of appendicitis, but the pain for appendicitis was associated with radiating to the right, not the left.

She bent down and whispered in Drew's ear. 'Okay, I know I'm a lady doctor but I need to have a little check of your testicles. Do you know what they are?'

He shook his head.

She lifted her eyebrows. 'Your balls.'

He gave a little giggle.

She nodded. 'All I'm going to do is have a little feel to make sure they are where they're supposed to be. It will only take a few seconds, and it won't hurt, okay?'

He nodded and she checked quickly. It was important with boys to rule out a twisting of the testes, but everything seemed fine.

She did another few tests, one—the McBurney's—the classic indicator of appendicitis. But nothing was conclusive.

Drew's guarding was evident. Something was definitely going on.

The nurse appeared at her side. 'Drew's blood tests are back. They're on the system.'

Jessica gave a nod. No wonder the junior doctor had been puzzled. *She* was puzzled. 'Let's get an IV up on Drew and I'm going to order an abdominal ultrasound to see if we can get a better idea of what's going on.'

She walked over to the nearest computer and pulled up Drew's blood results. His white-cell count was up, just as expected in appendicitis. She gave a little nod of approval as she saw the junior doctor had grouped and cross-matched his blood too, in case surgery was needed at a later time.

She looked over at Drew again. He was curled up in a ball, guarding his stomach like a little old man. And the strangest feeling came over her.

She unhooked her pink stethoscope from her neck. 'Drew, I'm just going to have a listen to your chest. It will only take a few seconds.'

She placed her stethoscope on his chest, waited a few seconds then took a deep breath and repositioned it.

She looked sideways at Callum. 'Has Drew ever had a chest X-ray?'

He shook his head. 'I don't think so. He's never had any problems with his chest. Why? What's wrong?'

Jess signalled to the A and E nurse. 'Can you arrange a portable chest film for me—right away?'

The nurse nodded and disappeared for a few minutes. There was always a portable X-ray machine in the emergency department.

Callum walked over to her. 'What is it?'

She placed her hand on his chest. 'Give me a minute. I

need to check something.' She wrinkled her nose. 'Have you ever had a chest X-ray?'

He rolled his eyes. 'Jess, I'm a fireman. I spent years working with a regular fire crew. Every time I came out of a burning building I had a chest X-ray.'

She nodded, it made sense, 'Right. So you did. And no one ever mentioned anything?'

He shook his head. 'Are you going to tell me what's going on? I'm going crazy here.'

She reached over and touched his hand. It didn't matter how upset she was right now. She'd even pushed aside the conversation she wanted to have with him right now. 'Callum, do you trust me?' Drew was the only thing that currently mattered.

His eyes flitted from side to side. Panic. Total panic. He ran his hand through his hair. 'Yes, of course I do, Jess. Why do you think I brought Drew here and asked to see you? There's nobody I trust more.'

The horrible reality right now was that she understood. She understood that horrible feeling of parental panic. That *out-of-control* sensation. She did. More than he would ever know.

She wrapped her other hand over his. 'Then just give me five minutes. Let me have a look at a chest X-ray for Drew. I promise, I'll explain everything.'

She saw his shoulders sag a little, saw the worried trust in his eyes.

She was telling herself that she would do this for any parent. That she *had* done this for any parent. But her conflicting emotions were telling her something else entirely.

The X-ray only took a few minutes and she pushed the film up onto the light box. It took her less than five seconds to confirm her diagnosis.

'Can you stay with Drew?' she asked the nurse.

'What is it?' The stricken look had reappeared in Callum's eyes, but she shook her head, pulled the chest X-ray down from the box and gestured with her head for him to follow her.

She opened the door to a nearby office and pushed the film back up on the light box inside. She flicked the switch and turned to face Callum.

'Drew has a condition called situs inversus.'

'What? What is that?'

She took a deep breath. 'It literally means that all his organs are reversed, or mirrored from their normal positions. Everything about Drew's symptoms today screamed appendicitis. Except for the positioning of the pain. Most people have their appendix on the right side. One of the true indicators of appendicitis is pain in the right iliac fossa.' She pointed to the position on her own abdomen to show him what she meant. 'But Drew's pain is on the other side—because his appendix is on the other side.'

'What does this mean? Is it dangerous? And how can you tell from a chest X-ray?'

She placed her hand on his shoulder. 'Slow down, Callum. One thing at a time.'

She pointed to the chest X-ray. 'Drew's heart is on the right side of his chest instead of the left. I can see that clearly in the chest X-ray.' She pointed at the lungs. 'I can also see that his left lung is tri-lobed and his right lung bi-lobed. That's the reverse of most people. This all gets a little complicated. It means that Drew's condition is known as situs inversus with dextrocardia, or situs inversus totalis.'

She tried to explain things as simply as she could. 'This is a congenital condition, Callum, it's just never been picked up. It could be that either you or his mother has this condition. It seems less likely for you as it would have been picked up in a routine chest X-ray.' She gave her head a little shake. 'It could be that neither of you has it. It's a recessive gene and you could both be carriers. Around one in ten thousand people have this condition.'

'Is it dangerous?'

She bit her bottom lip. 'It can be. Particularly in cases like this, when things can be misdiagnosed. But Drew's been lucky. Some people with this condition have congenital heart defects, but as Drew's been relatively unaffected that seems unlikely. It's likely if he had a congenital heart defect he would have had other symptoms that meant the condition would have been picked up much sooner. We'll do some further tests on him later. Right now we need to take him for surgery. His appendix needs to come out. How about we take care of that now, and discuss the rest of this later?'

He was watching her with his deep green eyes. She could see that he'd been holding his breath the whole time she'd been talking. He let it out in a little hiss. 'Will you do the surgery?'

The ethics of this question were already running through her mind. She had treated the children of friends on a number of occasions. It wasn't something she particularly liked to do—but in an emergency situation like this, the child's health came first.

'I'm the physician on call tonight. So it's up to me to perform the surgery. Would you like to find someone else to do it? That's always an option if you feel uncomfortable.'

He was on his feet instantly. 'No. Absolutely not. I want you to do it. I trust you to do it.' He looked her straight in the eye. 'There's no one else I would trust more.'

Things were still bubbling away inside her. It wasn't the time or the place, but she still had to say something.

'This isn't exactly ideal, Callum. And I'm not entirely comfortable about it. The surgery isn't a problem. There will be a registrar and an anaesthetist in Theatre with me. I'll need to go over the risks with you and get you to sign a consent form.'

She hesitated and let out a sigh. 'I kissed you a few days ago, Callum, so that complicates things for me. Obviously I didn't know about Drew...' she held up her hand as he tried to interrupt '...because you chose not to tell me. So, because I haven't met your son before, and don't have a relationship with him, that makes things a little easier.'

Her hands went to her hair and she automatically started twisting it in her hands, getting ready to clip it up for Theatre. She kept her voice steady. 'I'll perform your son's surgery and look after him for the next few days. I'll take the time to explain his condition and give you all the information that you need. After that? I have no idea.'

'Jess, please just let me explain.'

'No, Callum. Don't. Don't make this any more complicated than it already is. I've got more than enough to deal with right now.' She pointed back through the open door towards the curtains, where Drew was still lying on the trolley with a nurse monitoring him. 'Make yourself useful, go and sit with your son.' She walked out of the room, muttering under her breath, 'You don't know how lucky you are.'

Callum watched her retreating back and took her advice.

The nurse gave him a smile as he appeared back at Drew's side. 'You were lucky,' she said. 'Our Dr Rae is a fabulous paediatrician. Not everyone would have picked up that diagnosis.'

He gave a little nod. That didn't even bear thinking about. If he'd taken Drew elsewhere and some other physician had missed this...

It made him feel physically sick to his stomach.

He stroked his hand across Drew's forehead. His son

was a little more settled, the morphine obviously helping to a certain extent. Drew was the most precious thing in the world to him. He couldn't stand it if something happened to his son.

It was obvious he'd hurt Jessica's feelings by not telling her about Drew. And he wished he could take that back.

But it was too late now.

He'd explain to her later—once this was all over. He really didn't tell women about Drew. Drew was precious. He was a part of his life he kept protected, tucked away. And he had intended to tell Jessica about him. He'd just wanted to wait a little longer until he was sure they might have some kind of a chance at a relationship.

A relationship? Where had that come from?

He hadn't had a real 'relationship' since he'd broken up with Drew's mother. But Jessica was different. She was Jessica. His Jess. Someone he'd known a lifetime ago. And someone he hoped he could trust around his son.

Someone he could introduce to his son without wondering about other motives. Whether they might only really be interested in him, and not his son. Whether they might only be interested in dating a firefighter. Or some other crazy reason.

There wouldn't be any of that with Jess.

Jessica was a paediatrician. She must love kids. Why else do this job?

And she'd been interested in him when he'd been a pre-university student with no idea about his potential career prospects. So he didn't need to worry about that.

Drew opened his eyes and stared at him. 'Where did the nice lady go?' he murmured.

'She'll be back soon. She's going to make your tummy better.'

'Is she? Oh, good.' His eyelids flickered shut again.

He'd make it up to Jess.

He would. And he'd try to get to the bottom of the haunted look in her eyes.

He just had to get his son through this first.

Jess pressed her head against the cool white tiles in the theatre changing room. It was no use. She couldn't take the burning sensation out of her skin.

Thank goodness this place was empty. As soon as she'd slammed the door behind her the tears had started to fall.

It was so unfair. Callum had a son the same age as Lewis. Or the age Lewis would have been if he'd survived. A little boy he got to cuddle every day. To read stories to.

What kind of conversations did a five-year-old have with their parent when they were lying in bed at night, talking about their day?

A little boy he'd got to dress in his school uniform and photograph on his first day of school.

All the memories that Jess wished she had.

All the memories she'd been cheated out of.

Just when she'd thought she was getting better.

Just when she'd thought she could finally take a few steps forward.

Of course she had friends who had children the same age as Lewis would have been. She hadn't cut them out of her life. She couldn't do that.

She was a paediatrician, for goodness' sake. She couldn't spend her life avoiding children of a certain age. That would be ridiculous.

But sometimes it was difficult. And they were good enough friends to sense that. To know when to hold her close. To know when to give her a little space. It was a difficult path, a careful balance.

But this was different.

This was Callum.

An old friend, who was evoking a whole host of memories.

First Callum had appeared in her life. Then he had kissed her.

He'd raised her hopes, given her a glimmer of expectation that there might be something else out there.

And now this.

She was hurt. She was upset.

Upset that Callum hadn't told her about his son.

But the horrible coiling feeling in her stomach was something else.

She was jealous.

Jealous that Callum had a son and she didn't.

It was horrible realisation.

She'd seen the interaction between them. The stress in Callum's face when he was worried sick about his son. The slight tremor in his hand after she'd explained the surgery and the possible complications and he'd signed the consent form. The trust in his little boy's eyes, for him, and, more worryingly, for her.

She gave herself a shake. Children looked at her like that all the time.

The doctor who could make them better. The doctor who could take their pain away.

So why was it different that this was Callum's son?

An appendectomy was routine to her. Even though Drew's appendix was on the opposite side of his body. It shouldn't complicate the procedure for her. It was just a little unusual.

Maybe it was something else?

Callum was trusting her. Trusting her with his son.

And although she was worthy of that trust, it terrified her.

Because she knew what it was like to lose a child.

Other people in this world had lost a child. Other parents in this hospital had lost—or would lose—a child. She'd had the horrible job of losing paediatric patients and dealing with the bereaved parents herself.

But this felt very different.

No one in her circle of friends had lost a child.

She wouldn't wish that on anyone. Ever.

No parent should outlive their child.

No parent should spend the rest of their life looking at the calendar and marking off all the milestones that their child had missed.

She started to open packs and change, putting on a fresh set of theatre scrubs and tucking her hair up into the pink theatre cap. She had to get her head away from those thoughts. She had to get her head back into surgeon mode.

She walked through to Theatre and nodded to the anaesthetist, who was poised ready to start scrubbing at the sink.

Her registrar appeared at her side. 'I was just looking at the chest X-ray of the little boy for the appendectomy. Fascinating, I've never seen a case of situs inversus before—have you?'

She shook her head. 'No, I haven't.'

Alex started scrubbing next to her.

He was staring ahead at the blank wall as he started automatically scrubbing his hands, nails and wrists. 'I'll probably never see one again in my career. This might be interesting to write up.' He turned sideways, 'Can't there be complications in these kids? Heart defects and other problems? Some kind of syndrome?'

He was starting to annoy her now. He was clinically excellent, but a little too removed from his patients for Jessica's liking. In her book caring was an essential component of being a paediatrician.

'Yes, there can be a syndrome—Kartagener syndrome. People with situs inversus may have an underlying condition called primary ciliary dyskinesia. If they have both they are said to have Kartagener syndrome.' She started scrubbing her nails with a little more ferocity. Just what she needed—a registrar who permanently thought the glass was half-empty.

She preferred the other approach—the glass half-full approach. Especially when it came to children.

'You know, Alex, I've got a really sick little boy out there. His dad only brought him to our A and E department because he's a friend of mine, and the GP has been fobbing off his son's symptoms for days.' She shook her hands to get rid of some of the water then started to dry them on a sterile towel.

'I'd like you to think about that before we start. I'd like you to stop thinking about this little boy as a case for a medical journal. Think about him as a little boy who loves playing football, watching cartoons and eating chocolate cereal for breakfast. Think about him as the light of someone's life. Because the patient comes before the disease in every set of circumstances.'

She pointed to the door.

'Out there we have a father who is worried sick about his little boy. And even though I've been clear with him and given him the rundown of the surgery and the complications, he's sitting out there right now, wondering if his little kid will have peritonitis, develop septicaemia or be the one in a million who will have a reaction to anaesthetic.'

The theatre nurse came over and held out her gown for her. She thrust her arms into the sleeves and snapped her gloves in place. 'So let's make sure that I don't have to go out there and give him any bad news.'

She glared at him and stalked over to the theatre table. You could have heard a pin drop.

She knew she'd been harsh.

She never acted like that at work.

And the staff in here all knew her personal set of circumstances. They understood exactly where she was coming from.

Harry Shaw, the elderly anaesthetist—who stood in as Father Christmas every year with his grey hair and beard—gave her a smile.

His voice was low. 'You can do this, Jess.' He gave a little nod of his head. 'It'll be a walk in the park.'

She watched as the trolley was wheeled in. She could only pray it would be.

# CHAPTER NINE

'Wow—just wow.'

'What are you talking about, Pauline?'

The sister from ITU gave her a smile and pointed behind her at the delivery guy, who could barely be seen beneath the beautiful spray of pink, purple and orange gerberas. Jess was on her feet in an instant, reaching up and touching one of the petals. 'Aren't they gorgeous?'

Pauline was quicker, pulling the card from the top of the bouquet. She spun it around. 'Hmm... "For Dr Jessica Rae."' She held the card next to her chest as Jess reached over to snatch it. 'I wonder who these could be from?' She took a few steps away. 'I'm guessing Mr Tall, Dark and Very, Very Handsome. Otherwise known as Callum Kennedy.'

Jess felt her cheeks flush. 'Stop it!' She grabbed the card, putting it into her pocket without reading it.

Pauline tutted. 'I'm disappointed. He's a member of the emergency services, he should know better.'

'Know better about what?'

Pauline waved her hand. 'That we don't allow flowers in ITU.'

Jessica accepted the huge bunch of flowers and gave Pauline a smile. 'But these flowers aren't for ITU, these flowers are for me.' She pushed open the door to her office and placed them on her desk. 'Wow. Where on earth did he get these at this time of year?'

Pauline stood in the doorway and folded her arms over her chest. 'Must have paid a pretty penny for them.' She turned on her heel and walked away. 'It must be love.'

Jessica's stomach plunged. 'No, Pauline.' She pointed at the flowers. 'These are just a thank-you for looking after Drew.'

'Honey, a thank-you is a bunch of flowers from a supermarket. An enormous bouquet, delivered by a courier, that's a whole lot more.'

Jess sank down into the nearest chair. 'Oh.'

'Oh? That's all you can say? Just "Oh"?' She sat next to Jess.

'What did the card say?'

Jess bit her lip. Did she really want to get into this conversation? She dug into her pocket again and pulled the card out. Pauline was right, this wasn't just a thank-you. And she had a sneaking suspicion what it might be.

She read the message.

This was gigantic apology *and* a thank-you.

'What is it?' Pauline leaned forward and touched her hand.

'It's an apology.'

'An apology? What's Callum got to apologise for?' Her eyes narrowed, she was automatically moving into protective mode.

'It's…it's awkward.'

'What's awkward about it?'

Jess let out a sigh. 'He didn't tell me about Drew. The first time I found out was when he brought him in with appendicitis.'

Pauline's mouth fell open. 'How long have you known this guy?'

'Since I was a teenager. But I hadn't seen him in thirteen years. And I hadn't kept up with what was going on in his life.' Her voice dropped. 'Just like he hasn't kept up with what's happened in mine.'

'You haven't told him?' Pauline's voice was incredulous.

'It hasn't come up.'

'Just like his son didn't come up?'

Jess put her head in her hands and leaned on the desk. 'This is a mess.'

'Yes. It is.' Pauline never pulled her punches. It was one of the things that Jessica liked best about her.

She placed her hand at the side of her face. 'So, this guy—who you used to know thirteen years ago—and you only met again a few days ago, and brought his son to A and E, even though he hadn't told you about him?'

Jessica nodded.

'He brought his sick son to see *you*.' She emphasised the word strongly. 'Even though he knew that might make you mad. Even though he knew you might have a thousand questions. It was more important that he thought about the health of his child and—after seeing you in action—brought him to see a doctor he trusted with the health of his son. Doesn't that tell you what you need to know?'

Jessica flopped her head back into her hands. Someone else saying the words out loud made it all seem so much more straightforward. So much simpler.

She felt Pauline's hand on her back. 'Jess, what is it that you want?'

'What do you mean?'

'I mean, what are you ready for? I thought it was time for you—time to take some steps and move on. Callum seemed like a good idea. But maybe he's got as much baggage as you do.'

'And if he does?'

Pauline rolled her eyes. 'You need to think about this, Jessica. What do you want?' She pointed to the flowers. 'Are you ready to accept Callum's apology and whatever else that might mean?'

'I don't know. I mean I'm not sure. I was hurt that he didn't tell me about his son.'

'And what about Drew?'

'What do you mean?'

Pauline moved her hand to her shoulder. 'Look at me, Jess. I'm going to ask a hard question. How do you feel about having a relationship with someone who has a son?'

Jess's head landed back on the desk. 'I don't know. I mean, I *really* don't know. Drew's lovely. He's a great little boy. I've spent a little time with him on the surgical ward. He's made a good recovery and he's ready for discharge.'

'Is he ready for you?'

'What do you mean?'

'Do you and Callum actually talk to each other? Where's Drew's mother? She hasn't been to visit. She isn't named on the consent form.' Pauline dropped her voice and said almost hesitantly, 'Is she dead?'

'No. I don't think so. When I asked Callum to sign the consent he said something about Drew's mother being in America and him having full custody. I'm not really sure what happened there. I know she's been on the phone to the ward staff a few times every day.'

'Ah, so there's no other woman to get in the way?'

'Pauline!'

She smiled at Jessica. 'So what? I'm being a little mercenary. I have a friend to think about.'

Jessica's eyes drifted over to the flowers. They were beautiful and the irony of the blooms wasn't lost on her. Gerberas were her favourite flowers—had been for years.

She was surprised that Callum had even remembered that, but there was something nice about the fact that he had.

She stood up quickly. 'I need to go for a few minutes.' She looked about the unit. 'Is everything okay in here? Do you need me to see anyone before I go?'

Pauline shook her head. 'Everything's fine and, don't worry, I'll look after your flowers for you.'

Jessica rolled her eyes and hurried down the corridor. She glanced at her watch. Although the hospital allowed parents to stay with their children at all times, most parents went away for an hour or so each day to freshen up and change their clothes.

The surgical ward had been a no-go area for the last few days. Callum was there constantly with his son. Just as she would have expected.

She'd had to review Drew a few times every day. His recovery was going well and it was likely she would discharge him today.

But every time she'd been anywhere in the vicinity Callum had tried to speak to her. She'd fobbed him off as best she could. The flowers were the biggest message yet that he was determined to apologise and pursue this.

She just wasn't sure how she felt.

Her stomach churned as she walked down the ward. It was ridiculous. She spent all day, every day in the presence of kids. Why on earth would this little boy be any different?

Because he was Callum's.

Because this could be something entirely different.

If only she could be ready for it.

Drew had a little DVD player on his lap and was watching the latest Disney movie. Although he had his clothes on, the curtains were pulled around his bed and lights in the room dimmed. Most children who'd undergone an anaesthetic took a few days to recover fully. A nap time in the afternoon was common—and when most of the parents took their chance to go home, shower and change.

'Hi, Drew.' Jessica took the opportunity to sit down next to his bed. 'What are you watching?'

He turned the screen around to show her. She nodded in approval.

'So, how are you feeling?'

'I'm good. When can I go back to mini-kickers?'

She wrinkled her nose. 'Is that some kind of football?'

He nodded. 'I go every week with my friend Joe. I love mini-kickers. It's my favourite.'

'Well, we can't have you missing your favourite for long. Lie back and let me have a little look at your tummy.'

His wound was healing well. The edges were sealed and there was no sign of infection.

'This is looking great, Drew. The stitches that I used will disappear on their own. But you also have some stitches inside your tummy and if you do too much, too quickly, then it can hurt.'

'Tomorrow?' He was serious. His little face was watching her closely.

So this was how a five-year-old boy thought. Couldn't see past the football. There was something so endearing about that.

She laughed. 'No. Not tomorrow. Maybe two weeks—if you're feeling okay. Do you like school? Because if you do, it will be all right to go back to school next week.'

He wrinkled his nose. 'School's okay. I like school dinner. Mrs Brown makes the best custard.' He leant forward and whispered in her ear. 'The custard here isn't nearly as good.'

'Really? I always thought the custard here was quite good.'

He shook his head and gave her a look of disgust. 'Oh, no. Mrs Brown's custard is *much* better.'

He was a lovely little boy, with Callum's searing green eyes and a real determined edge about him. They were so alike she could have picked him out from a room filled with a hundred kids.

'What's your favourite subject at school?'

It was something that preyed on her mind from time to time. She'd often wondered what her own son would have enjoyed most at school.

'Dinosaurs or volcanoes.' Drew was absolutely definite about what he liked. He tilted his head to one side. 'And I quite like the sticky tray.'

'The sticky tray? What's that?'

'For making things. I was making a Christmas card for my dad a few days ago at school. I've picked blue card and I was sticking a snowman on the front.'

'Ah.' Jess gave a smile. 'What were you using for the snowman? Was it some cotton wool—like the kind we have in here?'

'Yes. It got kind of messy. The glue stuck to my hands and then the cotton wool got all puffy.' His face was all screwed up, as if he was remembering the mess he'd made.

Jessica leaned across the bed. 'It doesn't matter if you made a mess. I'm sure your dad will love it.'

'But I'm not finished yet. I still need to put some glitter on. I want to put some stars in the sky.'

'And that will be gorgeous, Drew. Then it's my job to get you back to school so you can finish it.'

Drew shook his head. 'That one got a bit messy. Can't you help me make another one?'

Jess hesitated. Everything in her head was screaming no.

She was a hospital consultant. She had a hundred other things to be doing right now.

But for the strangest reason none of them seemed particularly important. Here was an opportunity to do something nice. To do the first real Christmassy thing she'd done in...goodness knew how long.

She hadn't even put her Christmas decorations up for the last three years. It had hardly seemed worthwhile when she wasn't really in the mood. They were lying stuffed in a box in her loft somewhere. Maybe she should think about pulling them out.

She smiled at Drew. Yes, she could go and ask one of the play advisors to come and help Drew make a card.

But he had a really hopeful look in those green eyes.

How could she possibly say no?

She walked over to one of the play cabinets and pulled out a drawer. The hospital's own kind of sticky tray. She lifted up the vast array of coloured card and fanned it out like a rainbow in her hand. 'What colour card would you like?'

Callum strode down the corridor. He hadn't meant to be so long. But three nights of sleeping in a hospital chair did strange things to your body.

He'd stepped out of the shower and had only meant to sit down for a few seconds at home. The next thing he knew he had a crick in his neck and was hopping about the place, trying to get dressed in the space of five seconds.

If he was lucky, today would be the day he got to take his son home. And as much as he liked going to the hospital and getting to see Jessica every day, he'd much rather have his son safe at home.

He'd promised Drew's mother that they could Skype tonight. She usually did it every week with Drew and had been annoyed that she hadn't been able to see him while he'd been unwell.

It was just as well children were so resilient. Drew had seemed to get over his mother's abandonment within a matter of weeks. Probably because he'd been surrounded by people who loved him. But Callum could never forget the impact it had had on his son. What kind of a woman did that?

He turned the corner, ready to head into Drew's room, and stopped dead.

It was a sight he'd never expected to see.

Drew looked nothing like the child he'd been a few days ago, pale-faced and in pain. Today he had colour in his cheeks and sparkle in his eyes.

Drew and Jessica. Paint was everywhere. Cotton wool was everywhere. Glitter was everywhere, including smudged all along Jessica's cheekbones. But most importantly Drew was smiling, Drew was laughing. His attention was totally focused on Jessica. And the way he was looking at her...

It tugged right at Callum's heartstrings. Kirsten, his ex-wife, had never been the most maternal woman in the world. And since she'd left Drew had never really had a female presence in his life, that female contact. Sure, there were his friends Julie and Blair, and Julie was fabulous with Drew. But he didn't see her every day—didn't have that kind of relationship with her.

This was the first time he'd realised what his son had been missing out on.

He felt a sharp pain in his stomach. He'd always felt as if introducing Drew to any of his girlfriends would have been confusing for a little boy. Taking things a step too far. He wanted to protect Drew from all of that. And to be truthful he'd never been that serious about any of them. He couldn't stand the thought of different women yo-yoing in and out of his son's life.

Then there was that lingering dread of introducing Drew to another woman, only for her to change her mind and speed off into the sunset, leaving him to pick up the pieces.

But maybe he had been wrong? Maybe he'd been cheating his son out of so much more.

Jess seemed so at ease with his son. But, then, she should, she was a paediatrician, she loved kids. It was the field she'd chosen to work in.

It made him even more curious. Why didn't Jess have kids of her own? It was obvious she would be a natural.

It almost seemed a shame to interrupt this happy scene, but he had to. He wanted to know if he could take his son home. He cleared his throat loudly. 'What's going on in here?'

Drew's eyes widened in shock. 'Hide them, Dr Rae! Hide them!' He cupped his hands over whatever it was he'd been making.

Jess jumped to her feet and stood in front of the table they were sitting at, opening up her coat to block his view. She gave Callum a wink then turned her head over her shoulder towards Drew. 'It's okay. He can't see a thing. Put them in the envelopes now.'

There was the loud sound of shuffling behind Jessica's back, along with little-boy squeals of excitement.

But Callum was kind of stuck in the view right in front of his eyes. Jess was wearing a red woollen dress, which clung to her every curve, leaving nothing to his imagination. He was kind of glad that her white coat normally covered this view. He didn't want everyone else seeing what he could.

Jess sparkled. Literally. Blue and silver glitter along her cheekbones.

He lifted his thumb up and touched her cheek. 'You got a little something on here.' He brushed along her cheekbone then his fingers rested under her chin. He half expected her to flinch and move away, but she didn't. She stood still, fixing him with her deep brown eyes.

A man could get lost in eyes like that.

If he wanted to.

He stared down at his thumb. 'Is this a bit of a giveaway?'

She shook her head and glanced over her shoulder again. 'How are you doing, Drew? Nearly done?'

Drew held up two giant white envelopes, looking ever so pleased with himself. 'Done!'

He stood up, but stayed behind Jessica, putting his hands on her hips and sticking his head around. 'Wait till you see what I've made you, Daddy.'

Callum knelt down. 'I can't wait. I'm hoping we can go home some time today. What do you think, Dr Rae?'

Jess brushed her hair back from her face, leaving traces of glitter everywhere, including shimmering in the air between them. 'Oh, wow! I guess we went all out with the glitter, then.'

'I guess you did.' She was still smiling at him. Not avoiding him. And not avoiding Drew. Did this mean she'd finally forgiven him? She might give them a chance at... something?

'What do you think, Doc? Is Drew ready for discharge?'

He could almost see the silent switch—the move back into doctor mode. 'Yes, I think he is. His wound is healing well. We've done a few other tests—an ECG and an ultrasound of his heart. There's been no sign of any problems.' Her face became serious and the smile disappeared for a few seconds.

'Right now I'm assuming that Drew's situs inversus in straightforward. But I understand you might want to talk to someone about it. So, even though I don't think Drew will need any kind of follow-up, I've asked for one of the other consultants who specialises in genetic conditions to give you an appointment so you can discuss any concerns that you have.'

Callum pulled back a little. 'But why? Can't I just talk to you?' The words she was saying made sense, but that didn't mean that he liked them.

She shook her head. 'I don't think that's a good idea. I performed Drew's emergency surgery, but I probably have a conflict of interest here.'

He raised his eyebrows. 'A conflict of interest, what does that mean?'

'You know what that means, Callum.'

'But you must have treated a friend's kid before?'

She nodded slowly and stepped a little closer, lowering her voice and glancing in the direction of Drew. He'd become bored by their chatting and was now doing a jigsaw at one of the nearby tables.

'Yes, I have treated children of friends before—but usually only in an emergency. I wouldn't willingly be the paediatrician for any of my friends' kids. It crosses too many boundaries—complicates things and leads to confusion all round.' She tilted her head to the side and gave him a little smile. 'I'm sure you understand.'

'Actually, I don't.' He folded his arms across his chest. 'What do you mean?'

'Friends. Is that what we are?'

'Of course.'

He didn't like it. He didn't like it at all. It didn't matter that the concept of only being friends with Jess had circulated in his mind for days.

In the cold hard light of day he didn't like that.

He wanted more.

He wanted to be more than friends.

The kiss had started something.

No. That was rubbish. Something had started more than thirteen years ago.

There was unfinished business between them.

'What if I don't want us to be friends?'

Her head shot up. 'What?' There was that fleeting look across her face again. She was hurt. But she wasn't getting his implication. She was thinking he didn't *even* want to be friends. Not that he wanted something more. It was time to put that right.

He stepped closer and placed his hand on her hip. 'What if I wanted us to be more than that?'

Her pupils widened and her tongue shot out and licked her lips. Her eyes darted to the side, obviously to see if anyone was watching. He pressed his fingers a little more firmly into her hip, pulling her closer to him.

Drew hadn't even noticed what they were doing, he was still engrossed in his jigsaw.

'I'm not entirely sure what you mean,' she murmured.

'Truth be told—neither am I.'

His other hand settled on her other hip, feeling the wool under his fingertips, along with the outline of her hip. He still had to find out what was going on with Jessica. He was no closer to that than he'd been a few weeks ago. She played her cards close to her chest.

But Drew was happy. He'd warmed easily to Jessica. He liked her. She made him smile. And after what he'd witnessed today he was willing to take some baby steps.

'But let's find out.'

She lifted her hand and touched the side of his face, her hand trembling. She bit her lip. 'What if I'm not sure?'

'Then we take it slowly. We find out together. Are you willing to try that?'

His heart was thumping against his chest wall. An answer had never seemed so important. He wasn't even entirely sure what he was asking. This was all new territory for him. New territory for them both.

He glanced over at Drew. 'How about a date? A family date?' He'd never done that before. It wasn't just a step for him—it was a leap. But maybe now was the time to find out.

He could see something fleeting pass through her eyes. A moment's hesitation. Did she want to say no? Did she want to walk away?

There it was again. Her tongue licking her dry lips. What kind of effect was he having on her?

'Let's embrace the time of year. I promised Drew I would take him to see Santa at Cullen's Garden Centre in Largs on Saturday. They usually have a huge play park and real live reindeer for the kids to see. Do you want to come along?'

A nervous smile came across her face. 'A play park? Is that really a good idea after an appendectomy?'

He pulled her body next to his and gave a sexy smile. 'Oh, I think we'll be fine,' he whispered in her ear. 'We'll have medical supervision.'

The smile on her face seemed genuine now. 'I guess you will.'

## CHAPTER TEN

HER BEDROOM WAS a mess.

No, her bedroom looked as if a tornado had swept through it.

Every jumper and pair of jeans she possessed was scattered across her bed. Along with every raincoat, woollen coat, hat, glove and scarf. It was a beautiful eruption of colour, but Jess was still standing in her bra and pants. No further forward than she'd been an hour ago.

She picked up the phone next to her bed and pressed the automatic dial. 'Pauline? Help.'

Her friend sounded as if she'd just woken up. 'What is it, Jess?' she groaned.

'What do I wear?'

'Tell me you're joking.'

'No. Why?'

'You phoned me at this time in the morning to ask me what to wear to meet Santa?'

Pauline already knew about the date. She just didn't appreciate the agonising Jessica was doing over her wardrobe.

Jess sagged down onto the bed. 'Please, Pauline. Tell me what to wear.' She sounded pathetic and she knew it. This was the behaviour of a teenage girl, not a grown woman with a responsible job.

But Pauline's voice came through loud and clear. 'I would have thought that would be obvious, Jess. You're going to meet Santa—you wear red. Wear your Christmas jumper—the one you wore on the ward last year. Drew will love it. And your skinny jeans and your big red boots. There. That's you sorted. Anything else, or can a girl get back to sleep?'

The picture was forming in Jessica's mind. She hadn't even considered her novelty knitted jumper with the great big Christmas pudding on it. It would be perfect. She stood on tiptoe and yanked it out of the back corner of her cupboard. 'Thanks, Pauline. I'll see you tomorrow.' She hung up the phone and held the jumper in front of her for a second before quickly pulling it over her head. Pauline obviously had better vision than she did. The jumper, along with her skinny jeans and red chunky boots, was perfect. She even had a red coat she could wear too.

She glanced at the clock again. She couldn't believe she was this nervous. It seemed ridiculous. This was a simple trip—a chance to get out of Glasgow and have a nice drive along the Ayrshire coast until they reached the garden centre outside Largs.

She should be calm about this. She should be relaxed. She fastened her red coat and wrapped her scarf around her neck. The forecast today said it would be cold—really cold—so she wanted to wrap up warmly.

Her make-up was already on. Even though she hadn't managed to choose her wardrobe, when she did wear make-up it was always the same—some light foundation, some mascara and a little bit of red lipstick. It seemed to give her the little bit of colour she always lacked.

There was a toot outside and her heart leapt into her mouth. Oh, no. They were here.

Why had she agreed to this?

What if Drew decided that he hated her?

What if she just found this all too hard?

She walked down the stairs and sat on the bottom step for a few seconds, taking a few deep breaths. She could do this. She had *chosen* to do this. And she had to remember that.

No one was forcing this on her—no one.

Callum had lit up something inside her that had been dead for a long time.

And no matter how much she tried to deny it, it had felt good.

Then there was Drew. He was a gorgeous little boy. Being in his company was easy. With his big green eyes and determined manner it was easy to like him.

The fears she'd had about constantly comparing him to Lewis weren't there. Lewis was a totally different little boy.

She took a sharp breath. That thought.

She did that frequently. Still thought about Lewis in the present tense—as if he was still there. Did all mothers do that? Did all parents who had lost a child still think of their child in the present tense?

Was that good or bad? She wasn't sure.

Things were changing. She was changing. Yesterday she'd even pulled the box out of the loft with her Christmas decorations and tree. It had been hard to look at them again, the pink and purple globes brought back so many memories of previous happy Christmases in this house. So last night when she'd been shopping in the supermarket she'd bought a whole host of new decorations—silver ones. It felt different. It felt right.

The pink and purple ones held too many memories. The silver ones were new. With space available for memories of their own.

The car tooted again and she stood up, trying to ignore

the fact her legs were shaking. She stared at herself in the mirror in the hall, taking in the look of absolute fear on her face.

She picked up the fake-fur-trimmed hat on the table in the hall and stuck it on her head. 'You can do this,' she told her reflection. She closed her eyes for a second.

Harry Shaw's face drifted into her mind. The expression on his face that day in Theatre when she'd just been about to operate on Drew. *You can do this, Jess. It'll be a walk in the park.* And he'd believed it. She had been able to tell by the expression on his face.

She opened her eyes and stared at her reflection again, adjusting her hat in the mirror. She looked herself in the eye and repeated the mantra, 'You can do this, Jess. It will be a walk in the park.'

She gave herself a little smile then headed out to the car, pulling the door closed behind her.

Now, if only she believed that.


Callum's fingers were drumming nervously on the steering wheel. Drew was happy. He was watching his favourite DVD in the back seat of the car, oblivious to his father's tension.

Callum squinted at the address again. This was definitely the right number. And he was definitely in the right street. He peered at the front door again. It was lovely, white with a stained-glass panel. He was sure he could see movement behind it. What was taking Jess so long?

He looked up and down the street. This was definitely one of the nicest areas of Glasgow. The street was filled with well-kept town houses with private drives and neat gardens. Wouldn't a town house be a little big for a single woman?

He shook that thought out of his head as the door opened

and Jess came out. She was dressed in red today with a dark hat pulled over her ears.

There it was again. Even though he kept trying to ignore it. He was sure if they had him on one of those twenty-four-hour cardiac monitors his heart rate would shoot up every time he saw her. Jess was definitely wreaking havoc and adding to his chances of heart disease.

She gave him a little wave as she pulled the door closed behind her and started down the steps. Instead of walking around to the passenger side, she stopped and pulled open the rear door. 'Hi, Drew, how are you doing?'

Drew looked up from his DVD. 'Hi, Dr Jess. I'm good. Can I go to mini-kickers this week instead of next?'

She laughed. 'I can see five-year-old boys obviously have a one-track mind. I tell you what—let me think about it. Let's see how you do with Santa today.'

'Okay.' He pointed to the TV in the rear of the driver's seat. 'Do you wanna watch the dinosaurs too?'

She gave a little smile as she glanced at Callum. 'No, thanks. I'd better sit up front with your dad in case he gets lonely.'

'Aw, okay, then.' His eyes fixed on the screen again as she closed the door and walked around to the passenger side.

She slid in and started to unfasten the buttons on her coat. 'I was so worried about how cold it was going to be I totally forgot about the fact we'd be in the car for an hour.' She pulled her hat off her head, leaving her curls sticking up in all directions.

She seemed happy. She seemed relaxed and Callum felt himself heave a sigh of relief. He'd been so worried about this.

Worried that she'd change her mind.

Worried that she'd phone him and back out.

And although her face seemed relaxed, he'd noticed the way her hand was gripping her bag. Take things slowly. That's what they'd agreed.

He started the engine again and they pulled out onto the motorway, heading down towards Ayrshire. It was a bright day, with just a little nip in the air. Not quite cold enough to freeze yet and little chance of ice.

The road to Largs was always busy. It wound through various towns all haunted by a million sets of traffic lights, but the scenery made up for the slow-moving traffic.

'I didn't expect it to be so busy.' Jessica had leaned back in her seat and was changing radio stations for most of the journey. 'I thought people only went to Largs in the summer for the ice cream.'

He smiled. 'When was the last time you were in Largs?'

She frowned. 'I think I was a child. We were going to Millport for the weekend and had to get the ferry from Largs.'

'Did you get your picture taken on Crocodile Rock?'

She gave a little gasp. 'Hasn't every Scottish child got their picture taken on Crocodile Rock?'

He laughed. 'I've not taken Drew there yet. Maybe that's a trip for the summer.'

'What's Crocodile Rock?' came the little voice from the back of the car.

Jessica twisted round in her seat to talk to him. 'It's a rock that looks like a crocodile. Some people painted it red, white and black years ago and when I was a young girl everyone went to Millport in the summer and got their photo taken standing on Crocodile Rock.'

'But crocodiles are green!'

Callum tried not to laugh. Only a child's logic could say something like that. 'I'll show you some pictures of it later, Drew. I've got a photo taken standing on the rock. If you like it I'll take you over in the summer to see it.'

'Does it bite?'

'No, silly, it's a rock.'

Drew settled back into his chair. 'How far until we see Santa?'

Callum glanced at the road signs. 'About another ten minutes. We'll be there soon.'

'I'm hungry.'

'So am I,' Jess piped up. 'We'll get something to eat when we stop, okay?'

It was almost a relief to hear her say that. Even better was the sound of her stomach rumbling. It was like music to his ears.

She pressed her hand over it. 'Oops, sorry!'

It didn't take long to reach the garden-centre car park and Drew's DVD was instantly forgotten when he saw all the 'Santa's Grotto' signs. 'Look, Dad!' he shouted. 'They've got a sleigh and everything!'

He was out of the car like a shot and over at the painted barrier advertising Santa at the garden centre.

Jessica felt her stomach churn. He was so excited he was practically jumping up and down. It was so nice to see. So nice to experience. Lewis had been too little to really comprehend Christmas. Although he'd liked the presents, he'd still been a little scared of the man in the big red suit.

She felt Callum's arm around her waist. 'Everything okay?' Sometimes she felt as if he could almost read her mind. As if he knew when her thoughts were drifting off and taking her out of the present time and place.

She reached over and put her hand on his chest. 'I'm fine. I guess we'd better get in there before Drew bursts his stitches.'

They walked through the garden centre, past the blue-lit trees lining the driveway and fake snowmen and ani-mals. Inside the garden centre they had a path to Santa's Grotto and another to meet the reindeer. Callum went to the nearby desk to buy tickets. It was already getting busy in the centre, with lots of families and children arriving all the time.

The entrance was gorgeous. It was filled with a huge va-riety of pre-lit trees, sparkling in a variety of different col-ours. There were shelves and shelves of lighted ornaments, coloured parcels, little nativity scenes, sequin-covered trees and models of little Christmas villages playing music. On the surrounding walls were thousands of tree decora-tions, all hanging in different colour schemes to make se-lections easier.

All around the place children were squealing with de-light at seeing something new or squabbling over their fa-vourite tree ornament.

Jessica felt a little hand slip into hers. She looked down and Drew was staring up at her with anxious eyes. She knelt down next to him. 'What's wrong? Don't you feel well?' She couldn't help it, she was immediately moving into doctor mode.

He shook his head. 'I couldn't see my daddy,' he whis-pered.

Jess smiled. From down here, in amongst the jostling throng of people, it was hard to make anyone out, par-ticularly for a little boy who had been running to and fro between the attractions. But her bright red coat would be easily visible. When she stood up she could clearly see Cal-lum's back at the ticket booth, but she wasn't a little boy.

She slipped her hand out of her red leather glove and grabbed Drew's hand again. The heat was rising in the garden centre so she unfastened the zip on his jacket. It was even nicer holding hands, skin to skin. Drew seemed relieved to have found her. His immediate trust in her was so apparent.

Callum appeared next to them and waved the tickets. 'All the visits are timed. We can't see Santa until eleven-thirty. Want to get something to eat and then we'll go and see the reindeer?'

They nodded and followed him into the busy café. 'Have a seat, you two, and I'll get us some food.'

Jessica and Drew sat down at one of the nearby wooden tables. The whole café was decorated for Christmas with tinsel, garlands and Christmas holly wreaths hanging all round the walls. There was a cup filled with crayons on every table along with ready-made Christmas colouring sheets. Drew wasted no time and started to colour in a picture of the North Pole. 'Have you given your daddy your card?'

He shook his head. 'We posted the other one to mum in America. Dad helped me write the envelope. But I hid his under his pillow this morning.' Drew giggled. 'He won't find it until we get home.'

Jess smiled, watching Callum's back as he pushed his tray along the rack, picking up food as he went. He hadn't even asked her what she wanted to eat. She had a sneaking suspicion he was trying to feed her up. And she didn't feel insulted or annoyed. It was kind of nice that someone wanted to look after her.

The tray landed on the table a few minutes later with a glass of milk and a bacon roll for Drew, some toast with scrambled egg for her, and a full breakfast for Callum. He lifted some other plates onto the table with some home-baked scones, along with a caramel latte for Jess.

He really did have the best memory in the world. All the things in the world she liked.

'Okay, everyone?' he sat down in the seat next to Drew

and admired his crayoning. 'Let's eat and then we'll have a walk around the garden centre while we wait for our turn.'

Jessica looked around the room. It was full of families, all here either to buy a Christmas tree or pay a visit to Santa's Grotto. It had been such a long time since she'd been to a place like this.

She used to love visiting garden centres—especially around Christmas. She could easily have spent all her time off visiting one after the other, buying something in every place that she visited.

Something on one of the walls caught her eye. Little silver and red hearts, bunched together with bells to be hung from a Christmas tree. They were beautiful and just the sort of thing she would have picked in years gone by.

Callum followed her line of vision. 'Do you like them?'

She nodded slowly. A lump had appeared in her throat and she was too nervous to talk. She tried to clear her throat. 'I…I've changed my colour scheme. They would be perfect.'

He reached across the table and touched her hand. It was as if he knew. As if he'd just looked inside her head and saw that for a second she was struggling. 'Then we'll stop and get them before we leave. They look beautiful.' He took a sip of his coffee. 'Will your tree be red and silver this year?'

She shrugged. 'I bought some new silver decorations yesterday. I hadn't got much further than that.'

'Didn't you see the sparkly red ribbon near the door? It was on one of the trees.' Drew gave a little sigh. 'It was lovely.' Then he said quickly, 'But it's for a girl. It would be nice on your tree.'

'What colour scheme do you guys have?'

Callum choked on his coffee. 'You're joking, right? There's no colour scheme in our house. It's like a hotch-potch with every colour of the rainbow.' He smiled at Drew. 'Our colour scheme is whatever Drew's made at nursery or school that year. Right, son?'

Drew nodded and laughed. 'I've made lots of decorations. Daddy puts them all up on the tree.' He leaned forward and whispered in Jessica's ear, 'He says it doesn't matter if they're wonky.'

She felt a little tug at her heartstrings. She could just imagine their jumbled tree with haphazard decorations all made by a little boy. She wished hers could look like that.

Her silver and red decorations would seem drab in comparison. Suddenly the step she'd decided to take didn't seem nearly far enough. Not by a long shot.

She picked up a crayon and started to help Drew with his drawing. Callum's eyes were on her. He must have questions. But when could she tell him?

When could she tell him that there was a reason she wanted to take things slowly? It seemed almost deceitful when he'd invited her on a trip with his son.

He was still watching and smiling cautiously as he split the scones and put butter and strawberry jam on them. It was official. He was trying to feed her up. And he was doing a good job—it was the most she'd eaten in months.

But she didn't have the normal feelings she had around food. Mostly she was uninterested or dissociated herself from it. These last few weeks she'd started to notice the beautiful aromas of food again—instead of just the smell of coffee. In the garden centre today food smells were abundant. From the freshly baked scones and other cakes to the smells of bubbling soup, bacon and toasted cheese. Today was probably the first time in a long time she'd felt truly hungry.

'Is it time to go and see Santa yet?' Drew could barely contain his excitement and it was so nice to see.

Jessica stood up and held out her hand towards him. 'Why don't we go and see the reindeer? Maybe your dad will be able to take a picture of them for you. How cool would it be to show your friends at school that you met one of Santa's reindeer?'

Drew jumped up like a shot. 'Oh, yes, Daddy! Could I take it in for show and tell?'

Callum was smiling again and stood up. He looked at his watch. 'We've still got half an hour to kill. I think we can take some pictures of the reindeer.'

Drew sped down the path ahead of them, giving Callum a few seconds to reach and grab Jessica's hand. It didn't feel strange. It didn't feel unnatural.

Just as holding Drew's hand earlier hadn't felt unnatural. In fact, it had felt entirely normal.

An older couple was walking down the path towards them and stood aside to let Drew barrel past them. The older man laughed. 'What a lovely family,' he remarked.

Jessica felt herself catch her breath. Her feet were still moving, still walking down the path, but she felt every muscle in her body stiffen.

That's what they must look like.

A family.

An ordinary family.

She felt Callum squeeze her hand. He could sense it. He could sense her unease again. It must be killing him that he didn't know what was going on.

She so wanted to tell him. She so wanted to tell him right now before she burst into tears in the middle of Santa's Grotto.

Guilt was crawling all over her skin. Was this a betrayal? A betrayal of the memory of Daniel and Lewis—the people she'd thought she would spend the rest of her life with?

She could feel that horrible tight feeling spreading across her chest. Her breath was catching in her lungs.

Callum's feet stopped moving and his hand slid out from hers, turning her round to face him and sliding his arms around her waist. She couldn't lift her head to look at him. It was too hard right now as she was struggling to breathe.

This was wrong. Wasn't this usually the stage that single men ran away? When they heard someone mention something about a family?

Instead, Callum was taking it all in his stride. He pulled her a little closer and whispered in her ear, 'Just breathe, Jess. I don't know what's wrong, but this is a good day.' His voice was steady and calm. 'Wherever you are, know that I'm right here. Breathe.'

His hand rubbed gently up and down her back. A few people wandered past. Drew had raced on ahead and was out of sight. To the rest of the world it must just look as if they were taking a few seconds for a sneaky cuddle. Only Jessica knew the demons she was currently fighting in her head.

Gradually, the feeling across her chest started to ease. Her muscles started to relax. Callum released his grasp and pulled back, stroking her hair from across her face. 'Okay?'

She nodded. She didn't know what to say right now. How on earth could she explain what had just happened? What had caused that reaction in her?

He took her hand again. 'Ready to see some reindeer?'

It was as if he knew better than to ask right now. But even though his gaze was kind she could see the questions in his eyes. There was no judgement, only wonder.

She squeezed his hand. 'I would love to see the reindeer.'

They walked down the path to the outside stall where

the reindeer were. Drew was already standing agog. Of course none had a red nose, but the names of Santa's reindeer had been stencilled across the top of the stalls.

It was a wide paddock, with two members of staff—albeit dressed in elf costumes—on duty at all times. Jessica didn't know what she'd been expecting, but the reindeer seemed happy. They walked to the fence, and under the guidance of the staff allowed the children to stroke their coats and touch their antlers. They seemed healthy and in good condition.

Jessica had heard horror stories in the past about animals kept in children's play parks but it certainly wasn't the case here. In fact, the staff seemed enthusiastic, answering all the children's questions about the reindeer upkeep, with a few North Pole stories flung in for good measure.

'Can I get my picture with Comet, Dad?'

Callum nodded and knelt down as Drew posed next to the reindeer. Jessica waited until he'd finished then gave him a nudge. 'Go and stand next to Drew so I can take a picture of the two of you.' He obeyed and she snapped away happily. These would be great photos for Drew's show and tell at school.

'I want a picture with Dr Jess too!' shouted Drew.

Jess flushed. 'It's just Jess, Drew. You don't need to call me Dr Jess any more.'

Callum raised his eyebrows at her, obviously wondering if she would object to having her picture taken, but she swapped places with him and put her arm around Drew, letting Comet take pride of place in the background of the picture.

It was so easy to be around them. Drew had so much energy. No one would guess how sick he'd been a week ago. And Callum was every bit the doting dad that she'd expected him to be. It was so nice to see. And so easy to be a part of.

'Is it time yet, Dad?' Drew was bouncing up and down on the spot.

Callum looked at his watch. 'It's nearly eleven-thirty. Want to go down to the grotto?'

'Yippee!'

It was only a few minutes' walk. The path was lined with frost-covered decorations and houses. Christmas trees with green lights and gold stars lined the path, with red berry lights around the door of the grotto. Drew couldn't resist peering through the windows.

The garden staff had certainly gone all out to create a kids' paradise. They had staff dressed as elves, working away in a pretend workshop, piled high with sacks of toys. A little train ran around the outside of the whole complex with another elf driving it and children and parents in the carriages. 'Do we get to go on that too, Dad?'

Callum shrugged, 'I expect so.'

Jessica stood on tiptoe and whispered in his ear, 'I think that's part of the way out. Probably to make sure you don't stay in here too long.'

The queue moved along quickly and Callum showed Drew's ticket. An elf hurried over. 'Drew Kennedy? Come over here until we check and see if your name's in the naughty or nice book.' She held out her hand towards Drew.

His eyes widened like saucers and he turned to Callum, who smiled. 'Go on,' he urged.

'They asked me his name when I bought the tickets,' he said. 'They also asked me to choose which one he'd like best from a list of toys.'

'Wow. They've really thought of everything here, haven't they?' She looked around. 'You know, I'd love to bring some of the kids from the hospital here. You know, the ones that spend half their life stuck in a ward? Things are so well organised here, it could be perfect.'

'Why don't you ask before we leave if there's any way you can arrange it?'

She gave a little nod then nudged Callum. 'Look!'

Drew gave a little gasp as the elf pretended to find his name on the Nice list. 'Fabulous!' she shouted. 'That means we can go in and see Santa.'

'Come on, Dad. Come on, Jess,' shouted Drew as he tugged at the elf's hand.

Santa's Grotto was beautiful, filled with lots of fake snow and an icy blast of cold air. Santa was bundled up in the most padded costume and thickest beard Jessica had ever seen. And he had the patience of a saint. He took each child in turn, never hurried, never concerned about what was going on around him, and sat him or her on his knee, asking lots of questions.

Drew was totally enthralled. 'Tell me everything you want for Christmas,' Santa said with a wink towards Callum and Jessica.

Drew immediately reeled off a list of typical things a five-year-old boy wanted—a dinosaur, a racing car, a dress-up soldier's outfit. Then he stopped and pulled Santa down towards him, glancing towards his dad and whispering in Santa's ear.

Jess had a brief feeling of panic. Drew's eyes were on her the whole time he spoke to Santa. What was he asking for?

Santa smiled over at them both then spoke so quietly to Drew that neither of them could hear what he was saying. A few seconds later he handed Drew his present.

'Can I open it now, Santa?' he asked.

Santa nodded towards them. 'You'll need to ask.'

Drew jumped down. 'Can I, Dad? Can I?'

Callum swung Drew up into his arms. 'Say thank you to Santa and we'll go on the train. If you're good, you can open your present when we get to the car.'

'Yippee!' He squirmed around in Callum's arms. 'Thank you, Santa!'

They headed over to the train and Jessica laughed as Callum tried to squeeze his large frame into the carriage beside them. 'Budge up,' he said. 'It's a tight squeeze in here. This train is obviously designed for elves.'

The train ride was perfect. It started inside in the snow-covered landscape with snowmen and trees and wound its way outside to the garden centre, which was covered in a dusting of real snow and glistening in places with ice. The garden-centre staff had decorated huts to make them look as if they were still part of Santa's village.

After a few minutes the train came to a halt outside one of the buildings at the edge of the garden centre. It was a decorated barn. Jess and Callum looked at each other. They could hear the joyful squeals of children from inside. 'What on earth is in there?'

They waited as everyone alighted from the train, the elf standing at the front.

'Is there something else in there?'

The elf puffed out his already red cheeks. 'It's the winter wonderland—a children's playground.' He nodded his head at Drew. 'Your day's not over yet, pal.'

They walked inside and were hit with the wave of heat as soon as they crossed the threshold. The noise level was incredible. Every child who had visited Santa that morning had obviously ended up in here.

Around the edges of the playground were a variety of bedraggled parents sitting at tables, trying to make themselves heard above the noise.

Drew edged a little closer to his father. Jess knelt down next to him. The noise must be intimidating to a small child.

'Is there anything you'd like to go on?' she asked. Her eyes swept around the room and she put her hands on his shoulders. 'It's probably not a good idea to go on the trampoline or bouncy castle yet when you've had stitches in your tummy. But you could go over to the craft tables or into the games room if you wanted.'

Drew's hand slid into hers. 'Come into the games room with me.'

She nodded and gave Callum a smile as they made their way to the other side of the barn. He leaned over. 'This isn't like him. Normally he'd have made a beeline straight for the bouncy castle and dived straight on.'

Jess looked down at the little figure next to her. 'He's still in recovery mode. Being in hospital is a big thing for a kid. And having an anaesthetic takes a lot more out of them than you'd expect.' She rolled her eyes. 'Anyway, a bouncy castle or trampoline is the last thing he needs to be on right now.'

Callum gritted his teeth. 'Yeah, about that...'

'What?'

'I sort of bought Drew a trampoline for Christmas. He asked for it months ago and I bought it just the week before he was ill. It's sitting in the garage, waiting to be assembled. Am I going to have to say that Santa lost it?'

'What? No.' She shook her head. 'It's another few weeks yet. By then Drew should be fine. His stitches will be healed and he should be back to normal. But please tell me you've bought one of those big safety nets.' She waggled her finger at him. 'If you dare bring him into Casualty with a head injury because he's bounced off...'

He held up his hands. 'Whoa! No chance. With you on

duty and knowing the abuse I would get, I can assure you the safety net is ready.' He slipped his arm back around her shoulders as they headed into the games room.

He bent his head lower. 'Anyway, I remember the days when you weren't quite so safety-conscious.'

'What do you mean?'

He started to laugh and pretended to fumble in his pocket. 'Wait until I get the list out. First, there was the day you decided we should all jump into the harbour. Then there was the time you thought it was good idea to try out that thirty-year-old sled...'

'That was a family heirloom!'

He raised his eyebrows. '*Was* being the operative word.'

She stifled a laugh. Callum brought back so many good memories. Things that she'd forgotten about for so long. Things that she'd locked away inside the part of her mind that had stopped her from feeling joy any more.

It was so good to finally set it free again. It was so good to have someone to share this stuff with.

It was a bit quieter in the games room, with tables set with board games and a few electronic game machines. Drew didn't hesitate. He dropped Jessica's hand and raced off to watch the football game being played at the end of the room. Then he hesitated, turned round, took off his coat and hat and dumped them in her lap.

Callum pointed to one of the benches at the side. 'What do you say to another coffee? We could be in here for a while.'

'Sure. Thanks.'

The heat was building already. Jessica unfastened her coat and pulled off her hat and gloves. Callum disappeared to the coffee stand for a few moments and she leaned back against the wall.

Wow. So this was the stage Lewis would have been at.

Her eyes drifted around the quieter games room and then to the noisy throng outside.

Which room would he have wanted to be in? Would he have been in the thick of things, wreaking havoc outside? Or would he have been in here, like Drew, plotting his fantasy football side?

She let out a little laugh. How on earth did five-year-old boys know how to do that?

It was so nice to sit in here and watch all the kids at their various ages and stages. And even though she was thinking about Lewis, she was thinking about Drew too.

She watched as there was a minor clash of heads outside on the bouncy castle, and for the first time she didn't go into doctor mode and run forward to intervene. It was minor—their parents could deal with it—and she didn't want to leave Drew unsupervised. Callum had trusted her to watch over his son, even if it was only for a few minutes, and strangely she was enjoying it.

She hadn't been asked to come with them as a doctor. She'd been asked as a...what? A friend? A girlfriend? A potential lover?

All the things she would have immediately shied away from a few months ago. But with Callum it all felt so easy. One look from those green eyes and she tingled right down to her toes. One brush of his hand and her whole body craved more.

It was taking her time to get used to these feelings again.

To *admit* to feeling them.

To let herself feel them without being overwhelmed by sensations of guilt and betrayal. Slowly but surely she was starting to let those feelings go.

She thought about the photo currently in her living room. A beautiful photo of Daniel and Lewis, caught wrestling on the floor together, laughing together with unbridled pleasure. It was the image that stayed in her head.

Right there, caught in that moment of happiness forever.

They would always be part of her life—a wonderful part of her life—but the shades of grey around that picture were moving.

*She* was starting to move.

Starting to see a life past that.

'Jessica.' Her head shot up. Drew was waving her over. 'Come and see my score. I'm the top striker!' He was jumping up and down on the spot, clearly delighted. She ran over and gave him a hug. 'Well done, Drew, that's fantastic!'

He hugged her back with the exuberance that only a five-year-old could show. It felt good. It felt natural. It felt right.

Baby steps, her brain whispered. Just keep taking baby steps.

Callum walked around the edge of the winter wonderland with the two coffees, trying not to let his 'health and safety at work' hat annoy him. The coffee area should be cordoned off to minimise the risk of scalds to all the hyperactive children who were racing around the place.

He froze at the edge of the games room. Jessica and Drew were hugging in front of the giant TV, Drew obviously excited about something.

But that wasn't what made him freeze.

It was the expressions on both their faces.

Drew's was one of pure innocence and pleasure. The joy of sharing his delight with a mother figure. The way he'd wrapped his hands around her neck and was talking nineteen to the dozen in her ear.

And the way Jessica was looking at Drew.

Like he was the best thing she'd ever seen.

It had the strangest effect on Callum. He should be happy. He should be glad that his little boy felt so comfortable around the woman he hoped would be his girlfriend.

He should be delighted that they obviously had a mutual admiration society going. So many of his other friends had told him tales of woe about new potential partners and children not getting on—this obviously wasn't the case here.

But there was the weirdest feeling in the pit of Callum's stomach.

He knew there was something else. He knew there were parts of herself that Jessica still had to reveal to him. And it didn't matter what his memories of Jessica were. It didn't matter what effects one look of those brown eyes had on his body. It didn't matter how much he kept trying to push any little nagging doubts aside.

The fact was he wanted more. More than she was currently giving.

He wanted everything. The whole package.

Whatever that might contain.

But until he knew exactly what that was, he had a little boy to put first. He couldn't risk Drew's feelings or emotions. He could see the trust in his son's eyes. He could see the way he was already forming pictures in his mind—pictures that included Jessica.

Those pictures were starting to form in Callum's mind too, but he had to be sure. He had to be certain about Jessica before things went any further. It didn't matter how much he wanted to kiss her. It didn't matter how much he wanted to hold her in his arms. After a few short weeks he knew exactly where he wanted this relationship to go.

Drew was reaching up, touching one of Jessica's curls and tucking it behind her ear as he talked to her. Jessica caught his hand in hers and planted a kiss on his palm.

That was what he wanted for his son. So much it made his stomach ache.

Jessica looked over and caught sight of him. She frowned, obviously seeing the expression on his face, and gave him a little wave. She ruffled Drew's hair and pointed back at the big screen before moving over towards Callum and taking the coffee from his hand. 'Thanks for that. What's up?'

'Nothing. Nothing's up.'

She tilted her head to one side. 'Are you sure? You looked unhappy.'

She was staring at him with those big brown eyes. *She was worrying about him.* The irony wasn't lost on him.

And she looked happier. She looked more relaxed than he'd seen her in a while. If he could forget the episode earlier, today would have been a perfect day.

There was a little sparkle about her, a little glow. Glimmers of the old Jess shining through.

She glanced over her shoulder to where Drew was engrossed again in his game. There was something different in her eyes, something playful.

She gave him a cheeky smile then grabbed his arm and pulled him round the corner, out of the line of sight of everyone. 'I wonder if I can make you feel better,' she whispered, then she leaned forward and wrapped her arms around his neck, rising up on tiptoe and kissing him gently on the mouth.

And at that precise moment all rational thought left the building.

# CHAPTER ELEVEN

HER PAGER SOUNDED again. It was the fourth time in the last hour, but she'd been stuck in Theatre, performing surgery on a very sick baby with a necrotic bowel.

She pulled her theatre mask and cap off as the tiny baby was wheeled out of Theatre and off to ITU. She'd probably spend most of the night there, but she had to answer this page first.

She couldn't believe how tired she was. It was weird. For the last three years work had been her sanctuary. A place of focus. A place where she didn't have time to think about anything else.

And things here were good. Marcus and Lily, the two children with hypothermia, had both made a steady recovery and been allowed home. All the children from the accident had now been discharged and would be looking forward to Christmas with their families.

Christmas with a family. Something she hadn't even thought about for the last few years.

But the last few weeks had been different. Spending time with Callum and Drew had brought a whole new perspective to her life.

Life didn't just revolve around the hospital any more.

She didn't just wake up in the morning and stay there for as long as possible, only going home when the nurses eventually flung her out, then falling asleep straight away for the next day.

Work wasn't the first thing she thought about when she woke up in the morning. That was usually Callum and his green eyes—or Drew and whatever event he was looking forward to at school that day.

It was amazing how differently she felt about things.

In fact, tonight she'd been almost sorry that she was on call. She'd have preferred to spend more time with Callum and Drew.

For the first time in three years she was actually looking forward to Christmas. To spending it with people she loved. To have a Christmas when the focus wasn't just on being alone but sharing the time with others.

There was still the odd moment where she felt guilty. Usually in the depths of night when the feelings crept up on her unawares. When little voices in her head asked if she really deserved a second chance at happiness.

After all, she'd had her happy-ever-after. She'd been married to the love of her life and had had a beautiful son. Why should she get that chance again?

Was it fair?

Slowly but surely Callum and Drew were edging their way into her heart. Even just thinking about them brought a smile to her face.

It made her try to push the other voices away. Push them away into some dark place where she wouldn't hear them any more.

Her pager sounded again and she picked up the phone. The sister in A and E answered straight away.

'Bad news, Jessica. It's Grace Flynn. She's been admitted again. Her bloods have come back whilst we've been paging you—they're awful.'

Jessica's heart plummeted. Grace was a long-term patient. A seven-year-old with a rare form of invasive bowel tumours. She'd operated on another tumour only a few weeks ago and things hadn't looked good.

Children with cancer always had a wide team of staff looking after them at Parkhill. Grace had a paediatric consultant, a specialist oncologist, herself with her surgical skills and a whole host of specialist nurses. Even though doctors weren't supposed to have favourite patients, she'd been treating Grace for so long that she couldn't help but let the little girl have a special place in her heart.

'Have you sent her up to the ward or is she still in A and E?'

'The registrar's seen her and sent her up to the ward while we were waiting for her blood results and ultrasound. She knew her and thought she'd be more comfortable up there.'

Of course. Javier, the Spanish registrar, was familiar with the case. He'd dealt with Grace on a number of occasions over the last year. 'Ultrasound? Is there a chance her bowel is blocked again?'

She heard the sigh at the end of the phone. 'Put it this way, after a conversation with one of the other consultants he gave her a bolus of morphine and set up a continuous opioid infusion.'

Jessica sucked in her breath. News she didn't want to hear. Not for a child.

'I'll go straight up now,' she said. 'I can review the test results when I get there.'

Jessica replaced the phone and hurried up to the ward.

It didn't matter that she knew this was inevitable for Grace. It didn't matter that the doctors, family and nurses had already had discussions about future plans for Grace's care.

Her frail little body couldn't go through another round

of surgery—or chemotherapy or radiotherapy. Her body had already taken all it could.

The best they could do for now was to keep her comfortable.

She pulled up the test results and her heart plunged when she saw them. Nothing was good. The blood results and ultrasound could only mean one thing. She read the notes that her registrar had written, the record of pain relief and a few further comments by one of the other consultants involved in her care and called in tonight.

There was nothing to disagree with. She would have done exactly the same things that they had done.

Grace's mum, dad and brother were sitting at her bedside, along with one of the other paediatric consultants involved in her care.

Jessica stood in the doorway for a second, trying to collect herself. She was trying to keep her professional face in place and doing her best not to cry.

Grace's mum looked up and rushed over, enveloping her in a huge, crushing hug. 'Oh, thank you for coming up to see her. I knew you'd come.'

This was breaking Jessica's heart. She had still had a tiny little glimmer of hope in her eyes—as if at any moment one of the doctors would suggest something different—something completely out of the blue that no one had thought of. But it just wasn't possible.

If there was any surgery in the world Jess could do right now to save this little girl she wouldn't hesitate. But it just wasn't to be.

Her eyes met Grace's dad's. They were strong, resolute. Resigned to their fate but determined to give his little girl as much as dignity as possible. He gave her the tiniest nod, but didn't move from his place, holding his little girl's hand.

Jess moved into the room and sat down in a chair in the corner. The lights in the room were dimmed and Grace's little chest was barely moving up and down.

Her heart was breaking. She was finding it difficult to think straight. The tension in the room was palpable. They all knew what was about to happen.

Parkhill was a children's hospital and the sad fact of life was that children did die. But it wasn't a common occurrence. None of the staff here were used to it. None of them wanted to be.

Every child's death impacted on every member of staff that worked here.

She felt a hand on her shoulder. Pauline. 'Sorry, Jess, but I need you in ITU for the baby.'

She nodded and stood up. She still had a job to do, no matter how difficult things were right now.

She walked over to the bed and stroked Grace's hair. There was a horrible pressing feeling in her stomach. She honestly couldn't do anything more for Grace, and there was a baby in ITU who needed her now.

But she couldn't just walk out of here and say nothing. This might be the last time she saw this little girl alive.

Then it came to her, the poem that she and Grace had made up one day Grace had decided she wanted to be a horse rider. It had been a wonderful daydreaming session, when Grace had decided the name and colour of her horse, where it would be stabled and how famous it would become.

Jessica bent down and whispered in her ear, 'Riding across the fields, the wind is in your hair, holding onto Cupid's reins, as if you don't have a care. Racing through the grass, and tearing round the bend, all on a magical mission, to reach the rainbow's end.'

She felt tears forming in her eyes. In Grace's daydream

that day she'd reached the end of the rainbow and found the mythical pot of gold. If only something like that came true.

She took one final look. One glimpse of the family that was about to be changed forever.

The walls were closing in around her. Suffocating her. She gave the family one final smile and left, her feet carrying her swiftly down the corridor before she unravelled any further.

Her phone beeped. Again.

She pulled it out of her pocket. *Drew and I are picking you up at nine a.m. to make sure you actually leave.*

She smiled. She was exhausted, both physically and mentally. The baby she'd performed surgery on had needed constant review throughout the night. It had been touch and go for a while. But finally, around six a.m., the little mite had seemed to turn a corner.

She rubbed her eyes. What time was it now? She looked around for the nearest window. Was it even daylight yet? Dark winter mornings were notorious in these parts. It was frequently still dark in the morning when kids were walking to school.

There was a smudge in the background of the window. The first few edges of a rising sun. She dug in the pocket of her scrub trousers to find her watch. Just before eight a.m. A feeling of dread crept over her. She knew where she had to go next.

Almost as if someone was reading her mind, the phone next to her started to ring. One ring tone instead of two. An internal call.

Pauline picked up the phone swiftly. 'ITU Sister Jones. Yes, yes. I see. I'm really sorry.' Her eyes skittered towards Jessica, who felt her stomach tighten. 'I'll let her know. Have they? Okay, thanks for that.' She replaced the receiver and turned to face Jess, her face grave.

Jessica felt sobs rise up in her chest. Pauline's arm quickly came round her shoulders. 'Jess, it's been a big night. You were in surgery for hours, then with Grace's admission and the time you've had to spend in here...' Her voice tailed off.

'I should go back down. Back down and see the family.'

Pauline shook her head. 'They've gone home. Grace's brother was exhausted and Grace's parents decided they had to go home. They'll come back later today to make arrangements. John Carson, the other consultant, is meeting them then.'

It made sense. They would be exhausted. It would have been the worst night of their life. And John Carson had been sitting with them last night. He knew them inside out and had been involved in Grace's care from diagnosis.

Pauline placed both her hands on Jess's shoulder. 'Go home, Jess. That's what you need to do.' She glanced at the phone that was sitting on the desk. 'Go home with Drew and Callum. It's the best thing you could do right now. It's what you need right now.'

She nodded. She didn't even need to say the words.

This had probably been the second-hardest night of her life.

She'd felt herself unravel at some points. Felt as close to breaking point as she'd ever been. The only glimmer on the horizon had been the one in her heart.

Three years was a long time to nurse a broken heart. To go home to an empty house. To feel as if there wasn't much reason to get up in the morning. To wonder if anyone would miss you if you were gone.

Thank goodness she'd met Callum again. With his

come-to-bed eyes and his sexy smile. The one that could stay in her thoughts for hours.

That tiny little black cloud that had still been hanging over her head needed to be banished forever. It was time to stop avoiding the subject and let him know why she found some things so hard.

She knew in her heart that he would understand. That he would support her. And that was all she could ever want. Spending time with Callum and Drew had become the most precious thing in the world to her. Something she didn't want to live without.

She gave Pauline a hug. 'Tell John I'll be available if he needs me.' She walked down the corridor and into the changing rooms. She didn't want to wait a minute longer.

If there was one thing she'd learned it was that life was too short. Life was for living.

There were only two faces in the world she wanted to see right now. And they both had a place in her heart.

Callum glanced at the clock. Two minutes to nine. Just as well this wasn't a school day. His fingers were tapping nervously on the steering wheel.

He couldn't work out why he was on edge. He just knew he was.

It was time. It was make or break.

He wanted this relationship to work. He wanted it to move on. But for that to happen there needed to be honesty between them.

He needed to know.

He needed to know what had happened in Jessica's life.

Drew had spent most of the night talking about Jessica. The glow in his eyes had told Callum everything he needed to know. His little boy had fallen just as hard as he had.

He watched the door of the hospital, willing Jess to appear, and finally she did.

She looked shattered. She obviously hadn't slept a wink last night.

Her coat was barely pulled around her shoulders and he could see her eyes searching the car park.

He gave the horn a beep and waved to her. Her face lit up and she hurried over. He expected her to jump straight in but she didn't. Instead, she opened the rear door, gave Drew a quick hug and dropped a kiss on top of his head.

'We've been waiting for you,' Drew said solemnly.

'And you've no idea how happy I am to see you,' she answered. Callum turned, watching as she enveloped Drew in another quick hug. She looked truly happy to see him—to see them both. He didn't know whether to leap for joy or let that little cautionary voice in his mind rear its ugly head.

She closed the rear door and opened the front passenger door, climbing in and sinking into the seat next to him.

'Hard night?' He could see the furrows in her brow, etching deep lines into her normally smooth forehead.

She gave a little sigh and a shake of her head, glancing across her shoulder at Drew. 'More than you can ever know.'

The words hung in the air between them. He could tell there was so much she wanted to say—but couldn't because Drew was in the car.

His little hand stretched over and touched Jessica's shoulder. 'Jess, are we going home now? Are you going to watch my movie with me? I've got my duvet on the couch for us. We can snuggle up.'

A wide smile spread across her face. Relief. Relief at the thought of getting away from the struggles of the hospital and spending the day with them. Stress free.

He felt his stomach clench a little more. Was he wrong

to do this today? To ask her about her past and to put her on the spot about their future?

Part of him wanted to leave it, to stay in this happy limbo they were in. It felt like a safe place. But deep down he didn't want a safe place. He wanted much more. He wanted to be able to shout from the rooftops that he and Jessica were together. He wanted to make plans for a future for the three of them together, as a family.

He wanted to wake up every morning with Jessica by his side.

He wanted to be there to support her through whatever had happened.

He wanted to be a family.

And the only way to do that was to get rid of the elephant in the room.

He pulled out into the Glasgow traffic and started along the street. It was after nine so the morning rush was dying down. 'Want to go somewhere for breakfast before we get home?'

She shook her head. 'A duvet day with a film sounds perfect. I don't want to delay that for a second.' Her stomach gave a growl. 'But I'm starving. Do you have any bacon at home?'

'Daddy! Give her the chocolate we bought her!' Drew's voice echoed through the car. 'We bought you your favourite, Jess.'

Callum smiled and reached across her, opening the glove box and pulling out the orange-flavoured chocolate. It had been her favourite years ago, and he expected it still was. He put the chocolate in her lap. 'That will keep you going until we get home. We stopped to pick it up on the way here.'

Silence. Absolute silence in the car.

He knew instantly that something was wrong.

Thank goodness Jess was sitting down because the colour drained instantly from her face and she looked as if she might pass out.

She swayed—even though she was sitting in the seat.

They were heading through the busiest part of town. There was nowhere to pull over and the traffic was a little heavier here so he needed to keep his eyes on the road.

'Jess? Jess? What's wrong?'

Was she sick? Maybe it was nothing. Maybe she was feeling faint because she'd been on her feet all night and hadn't had anything to eat. That would be just like Jess. Too busy to sit down for a few minutes and think of herself.

But he had the strangest feeling he wasn't even close.

'Stop the car.' Her voice was quiet, almost a whisper.

'What?'

'Stop the car!' This time she was definite.

He could see the flare of panic in her eyes. She absolutely meant it.

His head flicked from side to side, trying to see if there was anywhere to stop in the midst of the queued traffic. 'I can't, Jess. There's nowhere to go. You'll need to wait. What's wrong? Do you feel sick?'

'I'll get out here.' She flung open the door and jumped out of the car. Her bag was still sitting in the footwell of the car.

Callum was stunned. What on earth had just happened?

'Daddy? Where's Jess gone?'

'I don't know, Drew.' He looked frantically up and down the street in the direction she was walking, trying to find somewhere to pull over.

What on earth had gone wrong?

This was supposed to be a good day. How on earth could a chocolate bar cause a reaction like that?

All the nudging doubts he'd had about putting Jess on

the spot vanished. Drew looked near to tears, sitting in the back of the car hugging his toy to his chest.

Something had upset Jess but she, in turn, had upset his son.

He couldn't have that. He couldn't have that at all.

This was crazy. And he couldn't let it go on a moment longer.

He'd been wrong. He'd been wrong not to sit her down and ask her right away what was going on in her life.

He'd been blindsided by her. She brought back a whole host of good memories and feelings. He loved being around her. She was beautiful—inside and out. He could see that. Even in the times she tried to hide it away.

He wanted things to work out between them.

His heart twisted as he watched the forlorn figure scurrying down the street and a whole new sensation swept over him.

He loved her. He loved Jess.

Just like he had years before.

Only this was different. This was a grown-up kind of love.

One that realised that nobody was perfect and everyone had history. And in his heart he knew she felt the same way—about him and about Drew.

So what on earth had gone wrong? He had no idea what had just happened.

But the one thing he knew for sure was that he needed to find out.

She was going to be sick. She was going to be sick everywhere.

She couldn't think or see straight.

Her hand reached out and grasped the wall, trying to steady herself.

A woman stared at her on the way past. She looked horrified. Did she think Jess was drunk at nine in the morning? Because that's the way she felt right now.

Her hand was gripping something tightly, her knuckles blanched white, her fingers growing numb.

Her hand was shaking. No, her whole body was shaking.

She leaned over and retched, trying to ignore the people walking past and looking at her in horror.

Unravelling.

She'd felt like that earlier on—in the middle of the night when she'd known Grace was about to die. She'd felt as if she hadn't had the strength to be there, hadn't had the strength to do the job she was supposed to be doing.

And now this.

Her whole world had just tilted on its axis.

In an instant. In a flash.

She stared at her hand, willing her fingers to open.

All this over a bar of orange-flavoured chocolate.

She heard the thud of feet running along the pavement. Felt a hand on her back. 'Jess. What is it? What's wrong?'

She could hear it all. The confusion in his voice. The concern.

She should have told him. She should have told him before.

Then he would have looked at her in pity and walked away. Then she wouldn't have dropped the walls around her heart and let him and his son in. Then she would have stayed safe. Locked in her own fortress where nothing could penetrate her heart and leave her exposed to hurt again.

She should have told him before.

But that would have made it all real.

Not the fact that it had happened. Not the fact that her

husband and son had died. But the fact that she was telling him—telling him, as she prepared to move on with her life.

Because up until this point she hadn't really told anyone—she hadn't needed to. All her work colleagues already knew and bad news travelled fast, following you like a billowing black cloud. She was used to people whispering behind her then averting their eyes when caught.

Maybe this was what she deserved. Why should she get a chance at a happy ever after with a new family? Maybe she didn't deserve it.

All the doubts and feelings of guilt were rearing their ugly heads. How could she forget about her husband and son? How dared she?

Callum looked utterly confused. He bent down and picked up the bar of chocolate. 'You're retching over this?'

The look on his face said it all. He was at breaking point. She'd known for the last few weeks that Callum was holding back—stopping himself from saying what he wanted to.

She looked at the bar of chocolate in his hand. It must seem so pathetic, but it didn't feel that way to her.

'You don't understand—'

'You're right. I don't.' His voice was soft and he stepped closer to her, touching the side of her cheek. 'So tell me, Jess.' He glanced over at his car parked at the side of the road, where he'd left Drew on his own.

She couldn't bear to look. Couldn't bear to look at the little boy who'd won a place in her heart. Not while she felt so guilty. Frustration was building in her chest. She wanted to say so much but just couldn't find the words. They all seemed to get jammed in her throat. 'I lost them. I lost them this way.' She pointed to the bar of chocolate in his hand.

'Lost who? What way?' He looked totally confused.

'Jess, I want to understand. Really, I do. But I can't until you tell me. It's time, Jess. It's time there were no secrets between us.'

Her legs wobbled underneath her. They couldn't take her weight any more and she felt herself crumple. 'My husband. My son.' Sobs racked her body. The words were out. They were finally out there. For everyone in the world to hear. For Callum to hear.

'What?'

She couldn't stop. Now the tears had started they wouldn't stop.

She felt his strong arms on her shoulders. 'What do you mean, you lost your husband and son?'

He was crouching now, on the ground beside her. She looked up into his green eyes. He was totally thrown by all this. Probably knocked sideways.

Her voice was trembling. 'My husband Daniel and son Lewis were killed in a road accident.'

His shock was palpable. 'What? When?'

'Three years ago.' Her shoulders were shaking now.

He shook his head, his disbelief apparent. 'Why didn't you tell me, Jess? Why didn't you tell me something like that?'

She was panicking now. People in the street were staring at them. 'I couldn't find the words. I didn't know how to tell you. I didn't know what to say.' Her breathing felt erratic, every breath a struggle. Her voice dropped, her eyes looking towards the horizon. 'It never felt the right time.'

Callum shook his head. 'How could you not tell me something as important as this?'

'How could you not tell me about your son?' The words shot out instantly. In blind panic.

He reeled back, looking as if he'd been stung.

She saw him take a deep breath and get to his feet,

reaching over, putting his hands under her arms and pulling her up with him. He looked about him. 'This isn't something to discuss in the street, Jessica.'

People were staring. People had stopped what they were doing.

She looked over at the car. Drew's little face was pressed up against the window. He looked frantic and her heart went out to him. He had no idea what was happening. Just that something was wrong.

If she felt upset and confused, how must he feel?

The chocolate bar was on the ground at her feet. Tears welled in her eyes instantly. 'I can't do this,' she whispered.

'Can't do what?'

She put her hands out. 'This. Us.' She looked over at the car. 'Drew.'

She could see sadness mounting in Callum's eyes. He didn't understand. He didn't understand this wasn't about him and Drew. This was all about her.

She shook her head. 'You don't get it. You don't understand. Daniel and Lewis—they stopped to buy me my favourite bar of chocolate the night they died. They stopped at a shop just round the corner from our house.'

Her voice was breaking, trembling as she remembered, the memories rushing up so clearly and strongly, as if it had just happened a few hours ago. 'He sent me a text.' She let out a huge gasp of air. 'Daniel sent me a text saying they'd be five minutes late because they'd stopped to buy me chocolate.' She shook her head.

'The next thing I knew the sister from A and E came to find me. I was standing outside the hospital, waiting for them, wondering what was taking so long. She'd been phoned by Ambulance Control—the crew had radioed in once they knew who they were dealing with.'

Callum hadn't moved. He was still standing over her,

his face unreadable. She must seem like a crazy woman, but everything seemed so clear in her head.

'What did she tell you?' His voice sounded a little wobbly too.

She looked up at him. She'd never seen his green eyes so full of conflict. She couldn't imagine how he must feel about all this. She'd never wanted to hurt him.

She'd never wanted to hurt Drew.

She took a deep breath, every part of the experience as painful now as it had been then. 'She told me Daniel had been taken to Glasgow Cross and Lewis was coming to Parkhill.' She looked off into the distance. It seemed easier to speak when she didn't have to look at him. 'That was normal after a RTA. The kids always came to us.'

'And then?'

He reached out and touched her hand, giving it a squeeze, willing her to have the strength to carry on. She could see tenderness written all over his face. She could almost reach out and touch the hurt he felt for her.

She'd been terrified to tell him. Terrified he would misunderstand.

She'd been right.

She looked at him. The tears were gone now. This was the worst part. This was the part that almost killed her.

'It was too late for them both. They were both dead on arrival. I never got to say goodbye, Callum. To my husband or my son.'

There was something so final about those words. So final, because she was saying them out loud. Her voice continued automatically—because she needed to get it all out. She'd held it in for so long. She'd wanted to tell him, but now it felt as if someone had released the dam and it had to all rush out.

'None of the staff knew what to do when Lewis arrived.

It's so different when it's one of your own. Somebody else's child is just as important but you have an emotional detachment that allows you to do the job, not to think about the hopes, dreams and fears of that little person in front of you. And to a certain extent you need that. But when it's one of your own...' She met his gaze. 'The child of a friend, colleague or loved one. It's like the world stops turning. You can't function any more, autopilot just doesn't work.'

She wanted him to understand.

She needed him to understand. Because it related to why she couldn't find the words to tell him.

And he must understand it a little. He'd been the parent with the sick child.

How could she have performed surgery on Drew if she'd known him like she did now? How could she have got through that op?

He was watching her steadily. She could see the rise and fall of his chest. His words were hoarse. It was almost as if he was seeing the whole picture in his head. Feeling her pain. 'They didn't resuscitate?'

She shook her head. 'There was no point.' She couldn't hide the forlorn tone in her voice. 'I think both of them probably died at the scene. It was strange—I always thought if something like that happened I wouldn't be able to do that. That I would resuscitate for hours and hours, no matter how hopeless. But it was totally different. I didn't want my son disturbed. I didn't want people to touch him when I already knew it was pointless. I just wanted to hold him.'

She wrapped her arms around herself at the memory of it. 'Someone phoned Pauline and she came down from ITU. I held Lewis for hours. And Pauline held me.'

There was silence between them. She didn't need him to say anything—she didn't want him to say anything.

She couldn't imagine how he must be feeling.

Well, she could, but only in part.

She remembered exactly how she'd felt when she'd first heard about Drew. It had been a total bolt out of the blue. And this was much worse than that.

Callum looked deep in thought—as if a hundred different things were spinning through his mind at once.

He couldn't stop looking at his car, where Drew was. She wished she could read his mind. Know what he was thinking. He dug his hands deep into his pockets. 'So, what's changed, Jessica? You may not have told me this before but it was still there. Still circling in your head every day.'

She felt a single tear slip down her cheek. It was so hard to put this into words. She looked at the little face staring out of the car window towards her and it made her heart ache. She so wanted to hold him. She so wanted to take him in her arms and give him comfort. Because she loved him. She loved that little boy—just as much as she loved his father.

Callum's face looked more than confused—he looked numb. As if he was trying to work out where his place in all this was. She'd done this to him. It had been her.

It was all her fault.

She was hurting people that she loved. Again.

'You don't get it.'

'No, Jess. I don't get it.' He reached over and pulled her towards him. For a second they stood in the street, their heads bowed, their foreheads touching.

If she could, she would stay this way forever. With Callum holding her as if he could take all her cares and worries away.

Because this was killing her. She hated herself right now. She hated hurting those that she loved.

'It was my fault, Callum. Don't you see? It was my fault that Daniel and Lewis died. If they hadn't gone to get me that chocolate, they wouldn't have been on the road at that time. They wouldn't have had that accident.' She reached over and grabbed his hand from his pocket. 'Just like you did today. You and Drew.' She shook her head as fiercely as she could. 'I can't have that. I can't have that on my conscience. Something happening to the people I love because of me.'

He lifted his head from hers and reached up and touched her cheek. His hand was freezing. They'd been standing out in the cold for far too long. Trying to dissect their lives in the middle of the street.

She knew this was ridiculous. Everything about it was so wrong.

She'd been hurt before. She was desperate.

How could this compare to losing her husband and son? It couldn't. And yet it was hurting every bit as much.

She'd started down that road. The one that was going to lead her to a new life. She'd started to feel again.

She'd started to trust.

She'd started to love.

And there would never be anyone as perfect for her as Callum and Drew. She could never feel as much as she did now.

And it was disintegrating all around her. Slipping through her fingers like grains of sand.

Callum shifted on his feet. He looked over towards the car again and something must have clicked in his head.

'What age was Lewis, Jessica?' His voice was sharp, abrupt.

'He was two. He was just two.' She was confused. It was a natural question. But it didn't seem quite right.

His eyes darted to the car. 'So he'd have been the same

age as Drew is now?' There was something in the way he said it. As if he was having a different conversation from her.

Her heart squeezed. The whole host of thoughts that she'd had at first about Drew came flooding into her mind. The comparisons with her own son, which had all faded as the weeks had progressed and she'd got to know this other little boy.

'Yes. Yes, he would.' Why was her voice shaking? Why did she feel as if she'd just sealed their fate?

'Oh, Jess.'

It was the little gasp in his voice. The way the words came out. As if his world had just crumbled in on itself.

He shook his head, very slowly. Were those tears in his eyes?

His voice was trembling. 'This was never about us, was it, Jess? This was never about me and Drew. This was about you—looking for a replacement family.'

'What? No.' She shook her head. 'Not at all.'

But Callum had switched off. It was almost as if he'd detached himself. 'You don't love me and Drew, Jess. You love the *idea* of us.' He was shaking his head again. 'I should have known.'

She couldn't believe this. She couldn't believe his brain was thinking this way. But she was so undone she couldn't think straight.

'I need you to love me, Jess. *Me.* And I need you to love Drew. For who *he* is. Not just the thought of a replacement for your own little boy. My little boy's already had a mother who walked away from him. I can't expose him to that again. I need you to love Drew with your whole heart. Love every inch of him—and every inch of me.' He was shaking his head again. 'You've broken my heart, Jess—truly you have.'

'But I do love you, Callum. I do. And I love Drew too.' Even as she said the words they sounded desperate. Like the last-ditch attempt to save something that was already slipping through her fingers.

This was over. This was finished.

It didn't matter that she'd been the one telling him she couldn't do this any more.

Part of her had still wanted him to tell her they could make it. That they could still have a chance of something.

But it wasn't to be. This was all too much for him. He hadn't signed up for this. That much was evident.

Her heart was breaking all over again.

She couldn't look at him. It was just too hard.

'We've both made a mistake here, Jess. I wanted you to be something that you just weren't ready to be. And you wanted us to replace something that you've lost.' He bit his lip. She'd never seen him look so shattered. So resigned to their fate. 'Neither of us can do that.'

His voice was tired. 'Get in the car and I'll drop you home. It seems we both have a lot to think about.' He took a deep breath and touched her cheek one more time. 'I'm sorry about your husband and son, Jess. I really am. I'm sorry that things just haven't worked out for us.' He pointed over his shoulder. 'But right now I have to put the needs of my son first.'

He shifted slightly, blocking her view of the car. 'I want you to say something—anything—to placate Drew until we drop you off. Can you do that for me and for Drew?'

'Of course,' she whispered. 'I would never do anything to hurt Drew.'

'Too late,' he whispered as he turned towards the car and walked away.

## CHAPTER TWELVE

THE DOOR OPENED and Callum jumped about a foot in the air. Drew and his little friend walked through the door, football boots in hand.

'You're back already?' He rubbed his eyes. Hadn't he just sat down?

He couldn't believe it was that time already. Julie and Blair walked into the room behind the boys and Julie folded her arms across her chest.

'Boys, go up to Drew's room for ten minutes and play. I want to talk to Drew's dad.'

Blair gave a shake of his head as he crossed the room. 'Why don't I just start running the bath and put them both in it?' He glanced at Callum on his way past. 'You're in for it, mate.'

Callum straightened up instantly. Julie and Blair were two of his closest friends. He'd never had any problems with either of them. They'd been fabulous, helping him with Drew. But even though they had a good relationship, Callum knew that Julie wasn't a woman to be messed with.

He stood up and walked towards her. 'Is something wrong?'

She waited a second, tilting her head to listen for the sound of the boys' footsteps going up the stairs and out of earshot.

'You...' She pushed her sharp finger into the middle of his chest. 'You're what's wrong. Kitchen. Now.' She turned on her heel and walked through to his kitchen.

'Ouch.' Callum rubbed the middle of his chest and started to follow her. He had a sinking feeling Blair had known exactly what he was doing when he disappeared with the boys.

Julie knew her way around the house. The coffee machine—which was only used on special occasions—was sitting on the counter and filled with water. She switched it on and turned to face him, folding her arms across her chest again.

'Right. Spill.'

Callum sat down on one of the breakfast bar stools. 'Spill what?'

She threw her hands up. 'You're the one sitting in a dark living room, staring at Christmas-tree lights. Tell me, how long were you there for? One hour? Two?'

Yeah, the Christmas-tree lights. The hotch-potch of decorations, along with the new silver and red ones that Drew and Jessica had picked out at the garden centre. Another reminder of Jessica. Along with the picture of the three of them Drew had drawn at school that was currently stuck to the fridge. Or the photo Drew had put on his bedside cabinet of him sitting on Jessica's knee at the winter wonderland.

Or the fact she was haunting his dreams. Every. Single. Night.

Julie was waiting. Waiting with her steely glare for an answer.

'I've had a hard few days at work. It's been chaos.'

'Pull the other one, Callum, it's got bells on.' She hadn't moved. The coffee machine was starting to bubble next to her.

'I don't know what you mean.'

She shook her head and started clattering around, pulling cups from cupboards and thumping them down on his worktop. 'I'm the one who's been in the company of your little boy. Your little boy who's missing Jess. She's all he'll talk about, Callum—well, that and some promise Santa made him.'

'Drew said something?'

She nodded as she put the coffee in the machine. 'Oh, Drew said a whole lot. All about some fight and how he wanted to see Jess and you won't let him.'

Callum put his elbows on the worktop and his head in his hands. 'It's difficult, Julie. I found out something about Jessica—and it's made me rethink everything.' He shook his head. 'But Drew's hardly said a thing. He's asked a few times if she's coming round, but that's it.'

Julie pulled the chair out on the other side of the breakfast bar and sat down directly opposite him. She counted off on her fingers, 'Apparently on Monday he asked if she would be coming for dinner, on Tuesday he asked if she could go to the pictures with you both. On Wednesday he asked if she would be here after his Christmas party.' She let out a sigh. 'Whether you like it or not, Callum, this is affecting your little boy.' Her face was deadly serious. 'What did you find out?'

He hesitated. He hadn't spoken to anyone about this. It felt like a betrayal. His stomach was churning at the thought of Drew remembering every day that he'd asked after Jess. Protecting him seemed more important than ever. 'She wasn't truthful with me. She didn't tell me something really important.'

'Like you didn't tell her about Drew until you had to?'

He cringed. It felt like a low blow. And it was just what Jess had said. But from Julie's mouth it had been a lot more sarcastic. He nodded and held up his hands. 'I know, I know, but that was different.'

'Different how?'

Blair hadn't been kidding. He was in trouble.

He shook his head and waved his hands. 'Her husband and son died in a car crash three years ago. She didn't mention them at all. She just told me things hadn't worked out for her.'

Julie's hand had shot up to her mouth. He could see her take a deep breath. 'So, how did you find out if she didn't tell you?'

Trust Julie to cut straight to the chase. 'Well, she did tell me. But it was out of the blue. After she reacted badly to something and said she couldn't do this any more.'

Julie screwed up her face. 'Are you trying to talk in riddles?'

'I told you—it's complicated.'

There came the sound of shouts and splashes from upstairs. She shrugged. 'I've got time.'

Drew felt wary. The things that had been circulating through his brain for the last few days were all on the tip of his tongue. The things that had given him a pounding headache and kept him awake every night jumbled around in his head.

'It was all over a chocolate bar.'

'What?'

He couldn't keep his exasperation in check. He stood up, almost knocking his stool over, walking over to the counter and pushing some pods into the machine and propping the cups underneath.

Julie stayed silent. It must be killing her, not breaking the silence. But he knew exactly why she was doing it. She was forcing him to say all this out loud.

He placed the coffees on the breakfast bar and sat down

again. 'I bought Jessica her favourite chocolate bar and I gave her it when we picked her up. After a few minutes she freaked out and jumped out of the car before I even had a chance to pull over. She said she couldn't do it. She couldn't have a relationship with me and Drew.'

Julie raised her eyebrow. 'Over a chocolate bar?'

Total disbelief was in her voice. She was waiting for the rest.

Callum sucked in a deep breath. 'Apparently her husband and son had stopped to buy her chocolate the night they had the accident. If they hadn't...' His voice tailed off.

'If they hadn't—what?'

'If they hadn't stopped she thinks they wouldn't have been killed. They wouldn't have been on that part of the road at that time of night. She thinks the accident was her fault.'

Julie sat for a few moments, biting her lip. She looked up from the coffee cup she had continued to stir. 'No. She doesn't.'

'What?' It was not what he'd expected her to say.

Julie sighed. 'Oh, Callum. This is much bigger than I ever expected. Tell me what else she said.'

He racked his brain. Did he really want to share everything Jessica had said? He'd been mulling over this for days. Going over and over things in his head. Maybe it would be useful to get another perspective.

He looked at the picture pinned to the fridge. 'It's all about Drew, Julie. This all comes down to Drew.'

'Why do you think that?'

'Her little boy—her son was the same age as Drew. If he'd lived he would be five too.' This was the hardest part. The part he hated most. 'She's looking for a replacement, Julie. She's looking for a replacement for her son—and maybe her husband.'

Julie looked shocked. She stood up sharply. 'Tell me everything. Did she say anything else to you that day? Anything at all?'

He winced. 'She told me that she loved me. She loved me and Drew and she couldn't put us in the same position her family were in. She didn't want to hurt us.'

'She told you she loved you?' Julie's voice rose.

He nodded and stared down at his coffee. He couldn't even bear to take a sip.

'She told you she loved you?' This time she was practically shouting.

'Yes. But it doesn't make a difference. She didn't mean it. It's not us that she loves. It's just the idea of us.'

Julie walked straight over to him, barely inches from his face. She looked furious. 'And what did you do then, Callum? What did you do when she told you that she loved you both?'

A horrible, cold sensation swept over his skin. Every hair on his arms stood on end. His actions had seemed perfectly reasonable at the time. He'd been so upset for her. And so upset for them too. He didn't want to be replacement for what Jess had lost. He wanted Jess to love him and Drew the way that they loved her—with their whole hearts.

'I told her to get in the car and say something to placate Drew. I told her I'd drop her off.'

'Oh, Callum.' Julie turned away. She put her arms up to her face and stood still for a few moments.

'What? I have to protect my son, Julie. Drew's the most important thing in the world to me. I won't let anyone hurt him. Not even her.' The words came spilling out. Why did he feel as if he had to defend himself?

'Drew's been through all this before. He had a mother who treated him as if he wasn't good enough. Who walked away from him. How can I put my wee boy through something like that again?' He shook his head. 'I can't. I won't.'

Julie touched his arm. 'But Jessica isn't Kirsten, Callum. Not by a long shot. From all the stuff that you've told me about her, they couldn't compare. Surely you know that?' Her voice was wavering.

And his heart started to pound in his chest. He knew what she was saying was true. He had just needed someone else to say it out loud for him. Jess was nothing like Kirsten. He knew in his heart of hearts that Jessica would never have walked out on her son. A thought like that would never even have occurred to Jess. She was made in a totally different way.

Julie spun back round and there were tears in her eyes. She pointed to the stool. 'Sit down.'

It was *that* voice again. Do or die.

He sat down numbly. Julie should be on his side. So why did he feel as if she wasn't?

'Callum Kennedy, you've been my friend for four years. You know I love you. But sometimes you are a complete git.'

'What?'

'When you're wrong, Callum, you're *so* wrong it's scary.'

He was starting to feel sick now. Sick to his stomach. She had that horrible female intuition thing, didn't she?

'What do you mean?'

She started pacing around the kitchen, her arms flailing around her. 'This wasn't about a bar of chocolate, Callum. This was *never* about a bar of chocolate. This was about a woman learning to let go and love again. She's scared, Callum—she's terrified. And with your reaction—frankly—who can blame her?'

'What do you mean, she's scared?'

'You and Drew—you're not a replacement family for her.' Julie looked at him in disgust. 'You could *never* replace her family, Callum.' She pressed her hand to her chest. 'They will always be with her—in here—forever. This is something totally different. Don't you see?'

He was starting to feel panicked. The last sensation in the world he ever felt. Not even in the middle of a fraught rescue. But he was feeling it now. His mouth felt bone dry. The lump in his throat was as big as a tennis ball. He shook his head. 'No. I don't see. Tell me.'

Julie reached her hands across the breakfast bar and clasped his. She looked at the drawing on the fridge. 'Callum, we both know how your son feels about Jessica. It's written all over his face. But how do *you* feel about her?' She pointed her finger to his chest again, this time a lot more gently. 'How do you feel in here?'

The million-dollar question. The thing that kept his stomach constantly churning because no matter what he did the feeling wouldn't go away. The words he didn't want to say out loud. Because then he would have to admit to a whole host of things.

Her pointed finger felt like a laser burning a hole straight through to his heart.

He looked up. 'I love her.' He could feel his voice breaking. But he didn't want it to. He took a deep breath and tried again. 'I love her, Julie.' This time the words were stronger—more determined.

It felt like a weight had been lifted off his shoulders. The acknowledgement of saying the words out loud. Admitting to himself and his friend how he felt.

Julie sagged back down into the stool opposite him. She put her elbow on the breakfast bar and put her head on her hand. 'Then what you going to do about it, dummy?'

# CHAPTER THIRTEEN

THE CANDLES FLICKERED around her.

They were beautiful, spilling yellow and orange tones along the pale cream walls in her house.

The Christmas decorations had been closing in around her. A permanent reminder of another Christmas alone. Sitting in the kitchen was different. The orange and pomegranate spice of the candles was soothing. She'd been trying some deep-breathing exercises. Anything to try and take her thoughts away from the constants on her mind.

Callum and Drew.

The door rattled then the doorbell started ringing and didn't stop.

'Jess? Jess, are you in?' The door rattled again.

Her heart started to race instantly. She recognised the voice. She'd recognise it anywhere. Something must be wrong. Drew. Something must be wrong with Drew.

She ran down the hall and yanked the door open. 'What is it? Is it Drew? Has something happened?'

Callum was stuck with his hand still in mid-air—frozen to the spot. It was almost as if he hadn't expected her to answer.

She looked down at the car parked at the side of the road. Drew wasn't in it. His car seat was empty.

Callum shook his head. 'No. No, it's not Drew. He's fine.' Then he paused. 'Well, actually, he's not fine.'

'What is it?' Her stomach was clenched. Was he in hospital? Had there been an accident?

Callum stepped forward, closing the gap between them. She could smell him. His distinctive aftershave was immediately invading her senses, bringing a whole host of memories. Bringing a whole heap of regrets.

He reached up and touched her cheek. 'He misses you. *We* miss you. That's what's wrong with Drew...' He paused. 'And with me.'

It was the last thing she'd expected to hear. She couldn't breathe. All her muscles contracted.

He put his hand on her shoulder. 'Jess, please. Can we talk?'

Her brain started to race. She was confused. She'd thought he hated her. The last time she'd seen him she hadn't been able to read the look on his face. Had it been confusion? Or resignation?

She felt overwhelming relief. Drew was fine. There hadn't been an accident. She couldn't help the way her brain worked. But, then, any parent would be the same— their first thought in a moment of panic would be for their child.

*Parent.* The word that had popped straight into her mind.

Her reactions to Drew were those of a parent. And her thoughts about Callum? She loved him so much it hurt to even be in the same space as him.

So, if this wasn't about Drew, why was Callum here?

She tried to focus. The messages between her brain and her mouth were getting muddled. There was so much jumbling around in there.

'Jess, can I come in?'

Her feet moved backwards automatically, creating space for him to come through.

He walked into the hall and glanced in the direction of the darkened living room. He took her hand and led her inside, bending down to switch on the lights of her Christmas tree.

Christmas lights. The ones she'd been trying to avoid. The new twinkling red berries and silver stars lit up the room. They had been her fresh start. But the chance to build new memories had been destroyed. All the tiny little hopes that had started to form. All the baby steps towards some new memories—like buying the new decorations with Drew—had been wiped out.

She was trying hard to focus. Trying to make sense of it all. Part of her was angry. This was the man she'd hoped for a future with. She might not have been truthful with him, but his reaction had still hurt.

'What are you doing here, Callum?' The tone of her words revealed the exhaustion she was feeling. Every bone in her body ached. She hadn't slept for days. She couldn't eat. The truth was she just couldn't go on like this.

His hands went to her waist and she gasped. His fingers were icy cold. It was only then she realised he wasn't wearing gloves or a jacket. Why on earth was he out on a freezing night like this with no jacket? Had he been in that much of a rush?

'I came here to apologise.' His voice was deep and husky. Was he being sincere? 'I came here to apologise for how I reacted the other day when you told me about your husband and son. I'm not proud of myself, Jess. I didn't understand.'

He was apologising. She felt shocked. Then she noticed the lines around his eyes and on his forehead. It was like a mirror image of her own face. Maybe Callum had had problems sleeping too. She shook her head. 'How could you understand? I would never wish something like that on you.'

'No. That's not what I meant.' He was babbling. 'Of course I don't know what it's like to lose a wife and child. But I didn't understand how you were feeling about us. Us—me and Drew. I got confused. I thought you were looking for a replacement. I thought you were using me and Drew as a replacement for your family.'

She pulled back. How could he think that? A million different things flew about her brain. 'But why? Why would you think that?'

Things started to drop into place. The questions. The expressions on his face. The age. This was all about Drew's age.

'Is this because Lewis and Drew would have been the same age?' For a second it felt as if someone had just dropped her back into the icy River Clyde. 'You think I would try and replace my little boy with another?'

No. It didn't even bear thinking about. How could anyone think that? She tried to keep calm. Sure, a few comparisons had swept through her brain. She'd even been a tiny bit jealous of Callum when she'd first found out about Drew. But to think she would try and do something like that?

She ran her tongue across her dry lips.

Wow. Maybe it wasn't such a leap in the dark. If the shoe had been on the other foot, might that have occurred to her? If she was the one with a child and Callum had lost his wife and child, would she wonder if he was trying to replace them?

Maybe. Just maybe. Even if it was only for a few seconds.

He pulled her closer, his chest pressing against hers.

'Jess?' He could see she was lost in her thoughts. He stared at her with his dark green eyes and she could see the sincerity on his face. 'I don't think that. I don't think that now. I was shocked. I never expected something like that had happened to you. I couldn't make sense of it in my head.'

It was easy. It was easy to feel his arms around her. It felt so good to sense him touch her skin again. But there was so much more to say. She couldn't expose her heart to this kind of hurt again. She wouldn't survive.

'Is that what you came to say?' She was trying to distance herself from all this. She could accept his apology—if that's what he wanted to offer. She could accept it, and then walk away. No matter how good it felt to be in his arms.

'No. That's not what I came to say.' He reached up and brushed her curls behind her ear. 'I came to tell you that I'm sorry. I'm sorry and I love you. Drew and I love you. I know I made a mess of this, Jess, but please don't give up on us. We want you to be part of our lives.'

'But—'

'Shh.' He put his finger against her lips then traced it over her cheekbones and eyelids. The feel of his light touch on her skin was magical. She could forget about everything else that had happened and just let this touch lull her into a false sense of security that everything would be fine.

She opened her eyes and took a deep breath.

'Don't say no. Please, don't say no, Jess. I can't be apart from you. *We* can't be apart from you.'

'But why, Callum, why now?'

'Look at me, Jess. I haven't slept in days. Neither have you—I can tell. This...' he waved his arms in the air '...is driving me crazy. I didn't mean to walk away. I just wanted to protect Drew. I needed to know that you were there because you loved *us*, not just the idea of us.'

'But how could you ever doubt that?'

He tapped his finger on the side of his head. 'Because I wasn't thinking straight. When you told me about your husband and son, I went into defence mode—protecting my son, protecting my family.' His hand cupped the side of her face. 'But you're part of my family now, Jess. You, me and Drew. I love you. I don't want to do this without you.'

She felt herself start to shake. From one extreme to the other. Callum was looking into her eyes and telling her that he loved her. Telling her that he and Drew loved her, Jessica Rae.

She wanted to believe him. She really did.

But ten minutes ago she had been wondering just how to get through one night. And even that had seemed too much for her. Even that had been taking candles and deep breathing.

'I...I...I don't know, Callum.'

He pressed his hand to her chest. 'How do you feel? How do you feel when you see me and Drew?'

There was no doubt. No doubt for her at all. It was the one thing that was crystal clear. 'I love you. I love you both.' But even as she said the words she felt fear and she instinctively made to pull away.

Callum lowered his head so it was level with hers—so he could look straight into her eyes. 'I know you're scared. I get that now. I can deal with that. *We* can deal with that together—as a family.'

She lowered her gaze. 'But how, Callum? When I saw that bar of chocolate it brought so many memories back. What if something happened to you and Drew? I can't go through that again.'

He gave her a smile. 'I know you're scared. But it's a big old scary world out there, Jess. You and I work in it every day. And what makes it all right is the people around us.' He took her hand and placed it on his chest. She could feel his heart beating under her palm. Thump, thump. Thump, thump.

'I can't promise you that everything will be perfect. I can't promise you that nothing will ever happen to any of us. I can't promise you that I'll never stop to buy you a bar of chocolate again. There are some things in this life we have no control over.' His other hand wound through her hair. 'What I can promise you is that I'll love you faithfully for every second that I'm here. I'll do my best to keep you and Drew safe. And if you have fears, talk to me about them. I'm here for you, Jess. I've waited thirteen years to get the woman of my dreams. I'm not about to let you escape now.'

Thirteen years. It seemed like a whole lifetime.

It had been a whole lifetime—for both of them.

'Can you give me a chance, Jessica? Can you give us a chance?'

He knew. He knew she'd been scared. He knew it had all felt too much for her and she'd needed some space.

But the love that she'd felt for Callum and his son had never faltered—not even for a second. Instead, it was growing, every single day.

'I'd like that, Callum,' she breathed. 'I'd like that very much.'

She could see the sparkle appear in his eyes. 'Then wait here.'

He turned and vanished, leaving her standing in the living room with only the red and silver twinkling tree lights.

She heard her front door open and some muffled voices then a little giggle. A little boy's giggle.

Callum appeared at the doorway with Drew standing in front of him, clutching something in a Christmas box.

'Drew!' She couldn't help herself, she rushed over and

hugged him as tightly as she could. 'I've missed you. Have you been a good boy?'

Drew was bouncing on his toes. 'Watch out, Jess. You'll squash your present. I made it specially.'

She turned to Callum, shaking her head in wonder. 'But how? The car was empty. Where was he?'

It was then she noticed. Under his thick jacket and hat Drew was wearing his pyjamas and slippers. Callum wasn't the only one who'd left the house in a hurry.

Callum gave her a nod. 'I have some good friends—they helped me out, in more ways than one.'

His finger brushed her cheek again and he knelt down on one knee opposite in front of her. Drew sat on his knee and held out the box. 'This might not be the most traditional way of doing things, but it probably suits us best.' Callum smiled at his son. Drew had a huge smile plastered to his face. 'We want you to marry us, Jess, and stay with us forever. We promise to love you, for now and for always. Will you marry us, Jess?'

Drew's little hands were shaking with excitement. She reached out and took the little red box, pulling off the lid and looking inside. Her hands were trembling. A few hours ago she had been feeling helpless and miserable, expecting to spend another Christmas alone, just wishing for it all to be over.

This was the best present she could ever have hoped for.

Her eyes squeezed shut for a tiny second.

She opened them again. Yes, they were still there. She wasn't imagining this. It was really happening.

She looked inside the box. There was one of the tiny Christmas decorations that she and Drew had bought together. A tiny little red heart. Except this one had been twisted on to some tin foil to make a ring. There was a little piece of folded paper next to it.

'I made it. Jess. Do you like it?'

She looked into their smiling faces. This was hers. This was her family. For now and for always.

'I love it.' She lifted the makeshift ring out of the box and put it on her finger, watching as it gleamed in the twinkling tree lights. 'It's perfect.' She gave Drew a kiss.

He pressed the little bit of paper into her hand. 'This is the real one we've picked for you. Daddy says it's a pink diamond because pink's your favourite colour.' He looked a little sad. 'But we couldn't get it tonight.'

Jessica looked at the printout. It was beautiful. It was breathtaking. 'It's perfect.' She smiled and looked at the little red heart. 'But every Christmas I want to wear this ring, because you made it for me.'

She put her hands around Callum's neck to meet his mouth with a kiss. She couldn't have wished for anything more. A family, not just for Christmas but forever.

Drew was standing at the fireplace staring at the chimney. 'Can I write a thank-you letter for Santa?'

Callum frowned. 'But it's not Christmas yet. You've not had your presents yet.'

Drew gave him a little knowing smile. 'Oh, yes, I have. Santa and I made a deal. He's just delivered his present early.'

Jessica linked her arm around Callum's waist. 'It seems our son has been making deals without telling us. What else do you think he asked Santa for?'

She could see the gleam in his eye. 'Let's hope it's a little brother or sister,' he whispered as he bent to kiss her.

\* \* \* \* \*

# ROMANCE

# MEDICAL

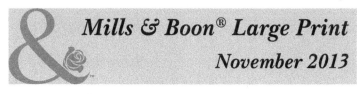

## Mills & Boon® Large Print
### November 2013

# ROMANCE

| | |
|---|---|
| **His Most Exquisite Conquest** | Emma Darcy |
| **One Night Heir** | Lucy Monroe |
| **His Brand of Passion** | Kate Hewitt |
| **The Return of Her Past** | Lindsay Armstrong |
| **The Couple who Fooled the World** | Maisey Yates |
| **Proof of Their Sin** | Dani Collins |
| **In Petrakis's Power** | Maggie Cox |
| **A Cowboy To Come Home To** | Donna Alward |
| **How to Melt a Frozen Heart** | Cara Colter |
| **The Cattleman's Ready-Made Family** | Michelle Douglas |
| **What the Paparazzi Didn't See** | Nicola Marsh |

# HISTORICAL

| | |
|---|---|
| **Mistress to the Marquis** | Margaret McPhee |
| **A Lady Risks All** | Bronwyn Scott |
| **Her Highland Protector** | Ann Lethbridge |
| **Lady Isobel's Champion** | Carol Townend |
| **No Role for a Gentleman** | Gail Whitiker |

# MEDICAL

| | |
|---|---|
| **NYC Angels: Flirting with Danger** | Tina Beckett |
| **NYC Angels: Tempting Nurse Scarlet** | Wendy S. Marcus |
| **One Life Changing Moment** | Lucy Clark |
| **P.S. You're a Daddy!** | Dianne Drake |
| **Return of the Rebel Doctor** | Joanna Neil |
| **One Baby Step at a Time** | Meredith Webber |

1013 GEN STD LP

## *Mills & Boon® Hardback*

### *December 2013*

# ROMANCE

| | |
|---|---|
| **Defiant in the Desert** | Sharon Kendrick |
| **Not Just the Boss's Plaything** | Caitlin Crews |
| **Rumours on the Red Carpet** | Carole Mortimer |
| **The Change in Di Navarra's Plan** | Lynn Raye Harris |
| **The Prince She Never Knew** | Kate Hewitt |
| **His Ultimate Prize** | Maya Blake |
| **More than a Convenient Marriage?** | Dani Collins |
| **A Hunger for the Forbidden** | Maisey Yates |
| **The Reunion Lie** | Lucy King |
| **The Most Expensive Night of Her Life** | Amy Andrews |
| **Second Chance with Her Soldier** | Barbara Hannay |
| **Snowed in with the Billionaire** | Caroline Anderson |
| **Christmas at the Castle** | Marion Lennox |
| **Snowflakes and Silver Linings** | Cara Colter |
| **Beware of the Boss** | Leah Ashton |
| **Too Much of a Good Thing?** | Joss Wood |
| **After the Christmas Party...** | Janice Lynn |
| **Date with a Surgeon Prince** | Meredith Webber |

# MEDICAL

| | |
|---|---|
| **From Venice with Love** | Alison Roberts |
| **Christmas with Her Ex** | Fiona McArthur |
| **Her Mistletoe Wish** | Lucy Clark |
| **Once Upon a Christmas Night...** | Annie Claydon |

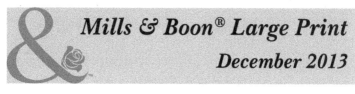

*Mills & Boon® Large Print*

*December 2013*

# ROMANCE

| | |
|---|---|
| **The Billionaire's Trophy** | Lynne Graham |
| **Prince of Secrets** | Lucy Monroe |
| **A Royal Without Rules** | Caitlin Crews |
| **A Deal with Di Capua** | Cathy Williams |
| **Imprisoned by a Vow** | Annie West |
| **Duty at What Cost?** | Michelle Conder |
| **The Rings That Bind** | Michelle Smart |
| **A Marriage Made in Italy** | Rebecca Winters |
| **Miracle in Bellaroo Creek** | Barbara Hannay |
| **The Courage To Say Yes** | Barbara Wallace |
| **Last-Minute Bridesmaid** | Nina Harrington |

# HISTORICAL

| | |
|---|---|
| **Not Just a Governess** | Carole Mortimer |
| **A Lady Dares** | Bronwyn Scott |
| **Bought for Revenge** | Sarah Mallory |
| **To Sin with a Viking** | Michelle Willingham |
| **The Black Sheep's Return** | Elizabeth Beacon |

# MEDICAL

| | |
|---|---|
| **NYC Angels: Making the Surgeon Smile** | Lynne Marshall |
| **NYC Angels: An Explosive Reunion** | Alison Roberts |
| **The Secret in His Heart** | Caroline Anderson |
| **The ER's Newest Dad** | Janice Lynn |
| **One Night She Would Never Forget** | Amy Andrews |
| **When the Cameras Stop Rolling...** | Connie Cox |